王烨　梁媛 等 编

新概念英语4

地道口语步步为赢

U0095768

中国水利水电出版社
www.waterpub.com.cn

内 容 提 要

　　本书囊括了生活中各种常用的英语句型以及对话，题材广泛，篇幅适中。以"你必须背诵的"强化读者记忆《新概念英语》课文中的经典口语表达；以"你一定熟读的"丰富读者的口语语境；以"你最好掌握的"教会读者常用的词汇、语法和固定搭配等知识点。全书编写层次由浅入深，循序渐进，方便读者学习和掌握。

　　本书适用于学习《新概念英语》（第 4 册）的读者。

图书在版编目（ＣＩＰ）数据

新概念英语. 4, 地道口语步步为赢 / 王烨，梁媛等编. -- 北京 ： 中国水利水电出版社，2010.7
ISBN 978-7-5084-7731-2

Ⅰ. ①新… Ⅱ. ①王… ②梁… Ⅲ. ①英语－口语－自学参考资料 Ⅳ. ①H31

中国版本图书馆CIP数据核字(2010)第142743号

书　　名	新概念英语4 地道口语步步为赢	
作　　者	王烨　梁媛 等 编	
出版发行	中国水利水电出版社	
	（北京市海淀区玉渊潭南路 1 号 D 座　　100038）	
	网址：www.waterpub.com.cn	
	E-mail：sales@waterpub.com.cn	
	电话：(010) 68367658（营销中心）	
经　　售	北京科水图书销售中心（零售）	
	电话：(010) 88383994、63202643	
	全国各地新华书店和相关出版物销售网点	
排　　版	贵艺图文设计中心	
印　　刷	北京市地矿印刷厂	
规　　格	145mm×210mm　32 开本　6.25 印张　220 千字	
版　　次	2010 年 7 月第 1 版　　2010 年 7 月第 1 次印刷	
印　　数	0001—5000 册	
定　　价	16.80 元	

前 言 Preface

　　《新概念英语》在当今的英语图书市场影响很大，成为一套风靡全球的经典英语教程，同时受到了世界各地英语学习者的青睐，也在中国的英语学习者中赢得了无可比拟的盛誉。1997年推出的《新概念英语》（新版）教程，更加注重对学生英语听、说、读、写四项基本技能的培养，更加符合中国英语学习者的特点和学习习惯。

　　很多人在学习新概念英语的同时，也期待能有一套同步辅导书帮助他们更好地理解掌握书中的内容，因此本套丛书也就应运而生了。

　　口语是衡量学生英语语言运用水平的主要标志之一，也是中国学生在学习中最容易忽视的部分，它在整个英语学习的过程中应占有特别重要的位置。

　　本书正是基于这种理念，根据《新概念英语》课文的难易程度编排相应的口语材料，所选材料涉及各个领域，同时提供大量精选短文和配套练习。它的最大特点是能够把课文经典句式、课外练习材料与重点口语词汇融合在一起，使学习者在提高口语能力的同时掌握更多更全面的知识。

　　本书采用符合学习者心理特点和逻辑思维方式的知识性材料，题材广泛，篇幅适中，极富启发性。它的核心点为强化训练，具体来说，本书对应《新概念英语》的每一课分为以下三个模块。

你必须背诵的

　　此模块立足《新概念英语》中的原文，精心挑选适合日常口头表达的地道句式，要求读者以英汉互译的方式，牢记这些经典的口语表达。

你一定熟读的

此模块对应《新概念英语》课文的题材和难度，为读者精选了丰富的口语情境。通过让读者熟读这些场景对话，激发学习兴趣，引起读者思考。所选材料的实用性极强，给读者营造模拟现场的氛围，让读者能身临其境地练习口语，增强记忆。

你最好掌握的

此模块对应《新概念英语》课文和课外口语对话，挑选出部分在口语表达和书面表达中常用的词汇、语法和固定搭配等知识点，并进行深度解析。

本书囊括了生活当中各种最常用的英语句型及对话，主题涉及的范围非常广泛，比如：家庭生活、休闲娱乐、接打电话、工作用语等方方面面，编写层次由浅入深，循序渐进，方便读者学习和掌握。

本书由王烨、梁媛编写，马云秀、王建军、王海娜、王越、白云飞、刘梅、张世华、张红燕、张娟娟、张静、李光全、李良、李翔、李楚、陈仕奇、罗勇军、姜文琪、董敏、蒋卫华等在资料收集和整理方面做了大量的工作，在此一并向他们表示感谢。

相信通过本套丛书的学习，能让读者更好地理解掌握《新概念英语》的教材内容，突破英语口语难关，步步为赢！

编　者

2009 年 12 月

目 录 Contents

Lesson

1

Finding fossil man

 你必须背诵的

发现化石人

我们从书籍中可以读到 5000 年前近东发生的事情，那里的人最早学会了写字。

但是，和我们相似的原始人生活的年代太久远了，有关他们的传说即使有如今也失传了。

石头是不会腐烂的，因此，尽管制造这些工具的人的骨头早已荡然无存，但远古时代的石头工具却保存了下来。

 你一定熟读的

情景模拟对话

A: Hello, everyone. Now we are in the Palace Museum.

B: Could you introduce its history to us?

A: Sure. The construction began in 1406 and it was regarded as the center of rule during the Ming Dynasty.

B: So how many emperors have been lived here?

A: A total of 24 during both the Ming and Qing dynasties. There are thousands of cultural relics exhibited in the Palace Museum.

B: That's fantastic! What are they?

A: Age-old jade artifacts, gold and silver ornaments, and paintings — just to name a few.

B: Wow. Those are really some of China's most priceless treasures.

A: Not just China's treasures, but the world's treasures too.

B: Yes, it is amazing.

A: 各位好。我们现在是在故宫博物院里。

B: 你能给我们介绍一下它的历史吗?

A: 当然可以。它始建于 1406 年,在明朝时被作为统治中心。

B: 曾经有多少位皇帝住在这里?

A: 明清共 24 位皇帝。故宫展出了成千上万件文物。

B: 真是太棒了!都有什么?

A: 远古玉器、金银饰品、名画,还有好多其他的展品。

B: 哇。它们真是中国的无价之宝啊。

A: 不仅是中国的财富,也是世界的财富。

B: 是啊,真是太棒了。

口语拓展

The pyramids were built by Egyptians under the orders of the Egyptian leader, whose title was pharaoh. There was a sequence of pharaohs culminating around 2615 B. C. , with the pharaoh Cheops who built the biggest thing ever built, the great pyramid, also known as Khufu. Cheops built a pyramid 770 feet on each side and 481 feet tall. How ancient builders managed to build these massive structures has never been fully answered but the effort clearly required brains and brawn.

The pharaohs may have set out to build magnificent tombs for themselves, but in the end they created monuments to human potential. There's a universal message in the pyramids. The pyramids belong to Egypt, but the pyramids also belong to the world. That's why we can all identify the pyramids as an early monument of human greatness.

金字塔是埃及人在他们的领袖（名为法老）的命令下建造的。在公元前 2615 年左右，几任法老相继统治埃及，基奥普斯法老建造了有史以来最大的金字塔——大金字塔，也被称为胡夫金字塔。胡夫金字塔边长 770 英尺，高 481 英尺。古代的建筑者是如何建造这些庞然大物的，这一直是个未解之谜，但很明显它需要付出大量的脑力和体力。

法老们的初衷是为自己建造豪华的陵墓，而最终他们创建的却是昭示人类潜能的纪念碑。金字塔蕴含着一种共同的信息，金字塔属于埃及，但它也属于世界。因此我们完全可以把金字塔作为展示人类伟大文明的早期纪念物。

你最好掌握的

1. emperor /ˈempərə/ n. 皇帝
2. dynasty /ˈdinəsti/ n. 朝代，王朝
3. relic /ˈrelik/ n. 遗物，遗产，遗骸
4. fantastic /fænˈtæstik/ a. 荒诞的，奇异的；极大的；极好的，了不起的
5. artifact /ˈɑːtifækt/ n. 人工制品
6. culminate /ˈkʌlmineit/ v. 达到顶点
7. massive /ˈmæsiv/ a. 大块的；可观的，大量的
8. magnificent /mægˈnifisnt/ a. 壮丽的，雄伟的
9. potential /pəˈtenʃ(ə)l/ a. 潜在的，可能的

Lesson

2

Spare that spider

不要伤害蜘蛛

我们要十分感谢那些吃昆虫的鸟和兽，然而把它们所杀死的昆虫全部加在一起也只是相当于蜘蛛所消灭的一部分。

人们几乎一眼就能看出两者的差异，因为蜘蛛都是8条腿，而昆虫的腿从不超过6条。

它们一年中消灭了多少昆虫，我们简直无法猜测，它们是吃不饱的动物，不满意一日三餐。

 你一定熟读的

情景模拟对话一

A: I was just watching a documentary on TV about people use dogs for various purposes. It was very interesting.

B: I love dogs. They have been used as guards for centuries. Nowadays, they are often used to find illegal drugs and bombs by the police and customs' officers.

A: The documentary also pointed out that they are used by shepherds to round up sheep and by rescue workers to find people trapped under rubble or snow.

B: Horses are useful to people too. We use them for sports and recreation.

A: Don't forget that horses are still used in many countries to pull ploughs and carts.

B: Can you ride a horse?

A: Yes, I can. I don't ride regularly though. How about you?

B: I can ride too. Perhaps we could go horse riding together at the weekend?

A: What a good idea!

A: 我刚刚在电视上看到一部纪录片,是关于人们养狗的各种目的,我觉得很有意思。

B: 我很喜欢狗。它们几个世纪以来被用来看门。现在,它们会经常被警察或者海关人员用来找一些毒品和炸药。

A: 这部纪录片同样指出它们被放牧人员用来驱赶羊群或者被救援人员用来寻找围困在瓦砾和雪堆里的人们。

B: 马对人类的用处也很大。我们在运动和娱乐上用到它们。

A: 也不要忘记了,马在很多国家里依然用来拉犁和拉货车。

B: 你会骑马吗?

A: 我会呀,尽管我不怎么骑。你呢?

B: 我也会骑,或许我们周末一起去骑马,你看怎么样?

A: 好主意。

情景模拟对话二

A: It's too hot. I'm not sure I can walk any more.

B: I want to go to Monkey Island and look at the monkeys.

A: What? They have a monkey island here? Really?

B: Of course they do. They have all kinds of monkeys here.

A: Great. Let's go. I love monkeys.

B: As for me, I've always loved boars and rhinos. I like their smell.

A: I wish we could get some good iced coffee somewhere. Wouldn't it be great if zoos had Starbucks in them?

B: Yes. Then I could buy you a few espressos and you'd climb over the fence into the lion cage.

A: Hah, hah, hah. Hey, look at that polar bear.

B: Oh, terrible.

A: Yes, I can't believe they have him out in the sun like this. Isn't it too hot?

B: It's sad. Sometimes I think zoos should treat animals better than they do. Look at the space they have him in. It isn't enough.

A: Yes, you're right. They should have him indoors in the air conditioning. They should give him a nice tank to swim in, and fresh meat every day. So where is that Monkey Island?

B: Over this way. Follow me.

A: 真是太热了，我不确定还能不能走。

B: 我想去猴子岛看猴子。

A: 什么？这儿有猴子岛？真的吗？

B: 当然有了。这动物园有各种种类的猴子。

A: 太棒了，我们走吧。我最爱猴子了。

B: 至于我呢，我一直很爱野猪和犀牛。我喜欢他们的味道。

A: 我希望我们可以从哪弄些不错的冰咖啡。如果动物园有星巴克咖啡店，不是很棒吗？

B: 对啊，然后我可以给你买一些浓缩咖啡，让你爬过栅栏进到狮子笼里。

A: 哈哈。嘿，看那只北极熊。

B: 喔，太过分了。

A: 对啊，我真不敢相信他们让它像这样在太阳底下，那不是太热了吗？

B: 真可悲，有时候我觉得应该对动物更好一点。看看他们给它的空间，根本不够。

A: 对，没错。他们应该让它待在有空调的室内，给它一处水槽游泳并且每天提供新鲜的肉。那么猴子岛在哪呢？

B: 在这条路，跟我来吧。

你最好掌握的

1 documentary /ˌdɔkjuˈmentəri/ *n*. 纪录片 *a*. 文献的，纪实的

2 illegal /iˈliːgəl/ *a*. 不合法的

3 regularly /ˈregjuləli/ *ad*. 定期地，有规律地

4 shepherd /ˈʃepəd/ *n*. 牧羊人 *v*. 看守，领导

5 round up 围捕

6 espresso /eˈspresəu/ *n*. 浓咖啡

7 polar bear 北极熊

Lesson

3

Matterhorn man

 你必须背诵的

马特霍恩山区人

现在登山运动员总想找一条能够给他们带来运动乐趣的路线来攀登山峰。

确实,在探险中他们经常遇到惊心动魄的困难和危险,而他们装备之简陋足以使现代登山者一想起来就胆战心惊。

阿尔卑斯山山区的小村几乎全是高山环抱、与世隔绝的穷乡僻壤。

 你一定熟读的

情景模拟对话

A: Xiang Shan is so pretty!

B: It's very quiet with a lot of trees. The red leaves make Xiang Shan more beautiful.

A: Do you often come here?

B: Yeah, we often climb Xiang Shan. Xiang Shan is not too high, so we always get to the top every time.

A: Mountain climbing is good for exercise.

B: Yeah, when I get to the top of a mountain, I feel so satisfied.

A: Well, let's have a match. I'll race you to the top.

A: 香山好漂亮啊！

B: 香山的树很多，所以特别幽静。红叶让香山变得更加漂亮了。

A: 你经常来这儿吗？

B: 嗯，我们经常来爬山。香山不是很高，每次来都会爬到山顶。

A: 爬山这运动不错。

B: 嗯，每次爬到山顶，总会有一种满足感。

A: 好吧，我们来比赛吧，看谁先到山顶。

口语拓展

The first and most famous of the climbers to disappear on Mount Everest was George Mallory. The British schoolteacher was a member of the first three trips by foreigners to the mountain. In 1921, Mallory was as a part of the team sent by the British Royal Geographical Society and the British Alpine Club. The team was to create the first map of the area and find a possible path to the top of the great mountain.

At the time, scientists believed that a person at the top of the mountain would only have enough oxygen to sleep. Scientists now know that two conditions make climbing at heights over eight-thousand meters extremely difficult. The first is the lack of oxygen in the extremely thin air. The second is the low barometric air pressure. Today, scientists say a person lowered onto the top of the mountain would live no more than ten minutes. Climbers can survive above eight-thousand meters because they spend months climbing on the mountain to get used to the conditions. Climbing to the top of Mount Everest is a major victory for any person.

在珠穆朗玛峰上消失的乔治·马洛里是第一个也是最有名的一位登山者。这位英国老师是第一位三次来到珠穆朗玛峰的外国人。在1921年，马洛里是作为团队的一份子由英国皇家地理学会和英国登山俱乐部派遣。该小组创建了这个地区的第一张地图，寻找可能到达山顶的路径。

当时，科学家们相信，在山顶的人，只会有足够的氧气睡觉。科学家现在知道两个条件使攀越8000米高空极为困难。第一是空气稀薄，氧气极为缺乏；二是低气压。如今，科学家说，一个人到山顶的较低的位置时，生存不会超过10分钟。登山者能够在8000米以上生存，是因为他们要花几个月的时间登山来适应那儿的条件。能够攀登珠穆朗玛峰的顶峰，对任何一个人来说都是重大的胜利。

 你最好掌握的

1. hiking /ˈhaikiŋ/ *n*. 远足
2. satisfy /ˈsætisfai/ *v*. 使满意，满足；达到（要求、标准）
3. royal /ˈrɔiəl/ *a*. 皇家的；极大的，庄严的，高贵的
4. oxygen /ˈɔksidʒən/ *n*. 氧气
5. extremely /iksˈtriːmli/ *ad*. 极其，非常
6. barometric /ˌbærəˈmetrik/ *a*. 气压的
7. survive /səˈvaiv/ *v*. 生存，幸存；比……活得长
8. victory /ˈviktəri/ *n*. 胜利

Lesson

4

Seeing hands

 你必须背诵的

能看见东西的手

她的视力与常人一样，但她还能用皮肤的不同部位辨认东西，甚至看穿坚实的墙壁。

维拉的特异功能引起了她家附近的一个科研单位的注意。

她穿着长筒袜子和拖鞋，能用脚识别出藏在地毯下面的一幅画的轮廓和颜色。

同时还发现，尽管她能用手指识别东西，但她的手一旦弄湿，这种功能便会立即消失。

 你一定熟读的

情景模拟对话一

A: So, you finally got your doctorate in genetics. Well done!

B: Thanks. Now, I have to find a job.

A: What are you thinking of doing?

B: I'd like to conduct some scientific research into genes. It would be wonderful to make a medical breakthrough.

A: There must be several private companies that are interested in employing someone like you. You could do some research for a university. There's a lot of discussion about genetics nowadays. Someone with you qualifications is bound to be in demand.

B: Many companies and universities are investing resources in genetics, because there are so many possibilities. Few people know where next discoveries will be made.

A: Well, I hope scientists don't decode to make a clone of me in the future! I wouldn't like to be the subject of an experiment.

A: 你在遗传学上获得了博士学位。祝贺你!

B: 谢谢,现在我必须要找工作。

A: 你想做什么呢?

B: 我想在基因上作一些科学调查。对产生医疗性的突破是很有好处的。

A: 那一定有一些私企对聘用像你这样的人感兴趣。你也可以在大学做一些研究。现在有好多关于遗传学的讨论。一些像你这样有资历的人注定是有需求的。

B: 许多公司和大学都在遗传学上投资资源,因为会有好多可能性。少数的人知道下个发现会在哪里出现。

A: 好吧,我希望科学家们不要将来对我破译进行克隆。我不喜欢成为一个实验品。

情景模拟对话二

A: What are you reading about in that science magazine?

B: There are several interesting articles on recent scientific break-throughs. I just finished reading one about cloning.

A: I'm not sure I like the idea of that. I don't want people copying me or other people. It could be very confusing.

B: According to the article, you have no real need to worry. Research nowadays is focusing on cloning parts of a human body to replace damaged or lost parts, not on recreating a whole human.

A: In the future, that could be possible.

B: In this article, scientists say that if you took the genes from someone and tried to create a copy of a person, there's no guarantee that the copy would look or act like the original!

A: Really? What else have you discovered?

B: I read about how scientists are using material from plants and animals to create new medicines. For example, an animal is immune to disease that affects human. So, scientists found out why it's immune and recreate that immunity for human.

A: That's great, because it uses natural materials rather than ones that scientists make themselves. I prefer natural remedies to man-made ones.

A: 那本科学杂志上你都读到了什么?

B: 在最近的科学突破性进展方面有些有意思的文章，我刚刚读到一篇关于克隆的文章。

A: 我不赞同克隆这个想法，我不想人们复制我或者其他的人，这会让人很混乱的。

B: 根据这篇文章，你没有必要去担心这个问题，最近的研究集中表现在把人身体内的克隆部分来取代损坏或丢失的部分，而不是去再创造整个人。

A: 将来就有可能。

B: 这篇文章说了，如果你从一些人身上获取基因然后尝试这复制另一个人，复制看起来或表现就像原本一样是没有保障的。

A: 真的吗? 你还发现了什么?

B: 我还读到科学家们从植物或者动物身上提取原材料来创造新的药物。所以，科学家们找到了为什么它是免疫的，为什么再次创造出对人类产生免疫的原因了。

A: 这很好呀，因为利用自然原材料总比科学家们自己制造出要好的多了，比起人类制造的治疗，我更倾向于自然治疗。

你最好掌握的

1 doctorate /'dɔktərit/ *n*. 博士学位

2 genetics /dʒi'netiks/ *n*. 遗传学

3 gene /dʒi:n/ *n*. 基因

4 breakthrough /'breikθru:/ *n*. 突破

5 qualification /ˌkwɔlifi'keiʃən/ *n*. 资格，条件，限制

6 bound /baund/ *n*. 跳跃，界限，范围 *a*. 受约束的，有义务的

7 confusing /kən'fju:ziŋ/ *a*. 使人困惑的，令人不解的

8 immune /i'mju:n/ *a*. 免疫的，免除的

9 remedy /'remidi/ *n*. 治疗法，补救，药物 *v*. 治疗，补救

10 original /ə'ridʒənəl/ *n*. 起源，原件，原稿 *a*. 最初的，原始的，独创的

Lesson
5
Youth

你必须背诵的

青 年

老年人和青年人只有一个区别：青年人有光辉灿烂的前景，而老年人的辉煌已成为过去。

他们既不追逐卑鄙的名利，也不贪图生活的舒适。

从某种意义上讲，他们似乎是宇宙人，同我们这些凡夫俗子形成了强烈而鲜明的对比。

青年人也许狂妄自负，举止无理，傲慢放肆，愚昧无知，但我不会用应当尊重长者这一套陈词滥调来为自己辩护。

你一定熟读的

情景模拟对话一

A: Hello! How are you today?

B: Hi. I'm feeling very nervous. I just had a test and I'm not sure how well or how badly I did.

A: It's no use worrying about it now. You've done test and you can't change any of your answers.

B: That's true. I really should go home and prepare for the next test, but I'm feeling tired.

A: Let's go and get a coffee together.

B: OK. I feel like sitting down and having a chat. How have you been recently?

A: Oh, you know me. I'm always happy! If I think I'm getting into a bad mood, I call some friends and socialize or have a chat.

B: That's a good idea. I usually just sit at home alone and get increasingly moody.

A: I hate spending too much time at home, I get bored of it. I'm always excited about going out to party or other social events and meeting people.

B: Perhaps I'm being too shy. I should always go out and not spend time worrying about tests!

A: 你好，今天怎么样？

B: 嗨，我感觉挺紧张的，因为我刚刚参加了一个测试，也不知好还是不好。

A: 你现在担忧根本就没有什么用，你都已经考完了，你也改变不了答案呀。

B: 你说得对。我真应该马上回家去准备下一个考试，但是我感觉很累。

A: 我们一起去喝杯咖啡吧。

B: 好，我感觉坐下来聊聊天挺好的，你最近怎么样？

A: 你知道我，我一直都很开心，如果我心情不好的话，我会给朋友打电话，交际或者聊天。

B: 不错呀，我总是独自呆在房间，情绪也是喜怒无常的。

A: 我讨厌在家消耗时间。我会厌烦的，参加派对或者社会活动，见一见朋友们，这样会让我很兴奋。

B: 可能我是个腼腆的人吧。我要经常出去，不要花太多时间用在担心考试的事情上了。

情景模拟对话二

A: Hello! What are you reading about in the newspaper?

B: Hello! I was exhausted from studying, so I decided to read the newspaper to relax. Unfortunately, the news is so depressing. There has been another murder in the city center. I'm shocked that the police haven't caught the killer yet.

A: People are starting to get frightened by it. Everyone will be relieved when they finally catch the murderer.

B: You mean "if" they catch the murderer. I'm scared stiff about going into the city center at night.

A: There must have been some good news in the newspaper. I can't believe that none of the news stories make you happy or excited.

B: Well, there was one good piece of news. You remember the local girl who was dying of a rare blood disease?

A: Yes. Her parents were raising money to have her treated in the united states.

B: Well, they've got the money and she's going tomorrow for treatment.

A: I'm so happy for the family! They must be very relieved and excited about that.

B: I'm sure they are. Oh, and a local man won the lottery. I'm so jealous! I wish it were me! I buy a lottery ticket every week and I'm amazed that I haven't even won a small prize yet. It's so unfair!

A: Don't be moody! I hope you're not tired, because we've been invited to a party this evening. I know how excited you get about parties.

A: 你好，你在报纸上读什么呢？

B: 你好，我学习学得太累了，所以我想读读报纸来放松一下。糟糕的是，这篇报道很让人压抑，在市中心有另一桩谋杀案，我对警察还未找到杀人犯感到震惊。

A: 人们都开始恐慌起来，我想大家只有在凶手落网的时候才会放松。

B: 你的意思是说"如果"他们抓到杀人犯的话。我想晚上去市中心时我会很害怕。

A: 报纸上一定还会有一些好的消息，我不相信没有一个好的消息会让你开心，兴奋的。

B: 嗯，这有一则好的消息。你记不记得那个得一种罕见血液病，快要结束生命的当地女孩子吗？

A: 记得。她的父母集资让她在美国去接受治疗。

B: 是啊，他们得到了资金并且明天就可以去治疗了。

A: 我真为这个家庭高兴。他们一定很高兴，也一定松了一口气。

B: 我也是这么想的。哦，一个当地人中乐透彩了。真让人嫉妒，我真希望那个人是我，每个星期我都去买，我很惊奇为什么我连一点儿奖金都没拿过，太不公平了。

A: 别不开心了！我希望你不会很累，因为我们今晚有一个派对，我知道你参加派对会有多兴奋！

你最好掌握的

1 exhaust /ig'zɔ:st/ v. 取出，用尽；使筋疲力尽；排气

2 depressing /di'presiŋ/ a. 令人沮丧的，令人沉闷的

3 relieve /ri'li:v/ v. 减轻，解除，缓和

4 scare /skeə/ v. / n. 惊吓，惊恐，惊慌

5 stiff /stif/ a. 坚硬的，严厉的，呆板的

6 socialize /'səuʃəlaiz/ v. 交际，使……社会化

7 moody /'mu:di/ a. 情绪化的，喜怒无常的

8 treatment /'tri:tmənt/ n. 治疗，处理，对待

9 jealous /'dʒeləs/ a. 嫉妒的

10 amaze /ə'meiz/ v. 使大吃一惊，使惊奇

Lesson

6

The sporting spirit

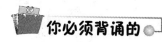 你必须背诵的

体育的精神

现在开展的体育运动几乎都是竞争性的。参加比赛就是为了取胜。

在乡间的草坪上,当你随意组成两个队,并且不涉及任何地方情绪时,那才有可能是单纯为了娱乐和锻炼而进行比赛。

但是要紧的还不是运动员的行为,而是观众的态度。

 你一定熟读的

情景模拟对话一

A: Aren't you interested in watching the Olympics? There have been some excellent performances by athletes from all over the world.

B: I never find it very interesting.

A: I think it's wonderful to see people from all over the world taking part in such a great event.

B: Oh, well. In my opinion, for a lot of people, it's just a way to show their country is better than other countries.

A: Yeah, but I think the Olympics can help to promote world peace.

B: I'm not sure about that. I think that the idea of the Olympics is good, but the reality is that during the Olympics from all the countries' competition, there's no real spirit of cooperation and people are usually not very friendly to each other.

A: You are so pessimistic! The Olympics is a great opportunity for athletes to demonstrate their speed, skill and strength. Most people hope to see someone from their country win, but I think that they are just happy to see good performances by any athletes.

A: 你不喜欢看奥运会吗? 会有来自全世界的运动员来上演精彩的体育盛事。

B: 我没发现它有什么意思。

A: 我觉得全世界的运动员来参加这样一次体育盛会是一件多精彩的事情呀。

B: 嗯。但我认为,对大部分的人来说,它只是一种展示他们国家比其他国家更有优势的形式。

A: 对,但是我认为奥运会能够促进世界的和平。

B: 我不这样认为。我觉得奥运会的想法是不错的,但是现实是在奥运会上是来自所有国家的竞争,没有真正的合作精神,而且人与人之间也不总是那么友好。

A: 你太悲观了。奥运会对运动员来说是一个展示他们速度、技能以及力量的好机会,大部分人都希望他们的国家能够取得胜利,但能看到任何一个运动员精彩的比赛他们还是很开心的。

情景模拟对话二

A: Are extreme sports popular in your country?

B: They're not very popular. Only a relatively small number of people do them. Many people enjoy watching them on TV. There's a very popular TV program on each week.

A: Which sports are usually featured on the program?

B: Bungee jumping, skydiving, and cliff diving are the most common, but there are other kinds of sports, such as motor racing and skate-boarding.

A: I think that the people who do the skateboarding are very skilled. It must be take a lot of practices to stay on the skateboard whilst doing so many jumps and turns.

B: The kids who do it are so young. Well, it's better for them than sitting at home watching TV all day!

A: Would you like to try any extreme sports?

B: I'm going to bungee jumping on Saturday. I'm very nervous about it, but my friends convinced me to give it a try.

A: I'm sure you'll be safe. The organizers have lots of safety procedures. Can I come and watch?

B: I guess so. You might even be tempted to do a bungee jump.

A: I might. It's something I've often thought about doing.

A: 极限运动在你们那儿受欢迎吗？

B: 不怎么受欢迎，只有一小部分人喜欢。更多人选择在家从电视里观看。每个星期这个节目都很火爆。

A: 都有什么样特色的体育运动？

B: 蹦极、跳伞、悬崖跳水都是很普通的项目。但是也有一些其他的运动，像是赛车和滑板。

A: 我看那些玩滑板的人技巧都很高。他们停留在滑板上同时还要旋转、跳跃，一定是花了不少的功夫练习。

B: 玩这个运动的孩子们都很年轻。这总比他们成天呆在家里看电视强很多。

A: 你想尝试极限运动吗？

B: 我想周六去蹦极。我挺紧张的，但是我朋友们说服我去试试。

A: 我保证你会很安全的。组织者有很多安全设施。我能去看看吗？

B: 可以去，我想你也可以尝试一下。

A: 我可能会吧，这也是我一直想做的事情。

你最好掌握的

1 cooperation /kəuˌɔpəˈreiʃən/ *n*. 合作，协作

2 pessimistic /ˌpesiˈmistik/ *a*. 悲观的

3 demonstrate /ˈdemənstreit/ *v*. 证明，演示，示威，示范

4 extreme sports 极限运动

5 participate /pɑːˈtisipeit/ *v*. 参加，参与

6 bungee jumping 蹦极跳，高空弹跳

7 skateboarding /ˈskeitbɔːdiŋ/ *n*. 滑板

8 convince /kənˈvins/ *v*. 说服，使……相信

9 safety procedure 安全程序，安全措施

Lesson

7 Bats

蝙 蝠

要透彻理解这句话的意义，我们应先回顾一下人类最近的几项发明。

固体障碍物越远，回声返回所用的时间越长。

任何固体都反射声音，反射的声音因物体的大小和性质的不同而不同。

你一定熟读的

情景模拟对话

A: What do you think of the way people use and treat animals?

B: I think most people treat animals well, but we are often cruel to animals. When we raise animals for food, the conditions they live in are often poor.

A: Perhaps people should stop eating animals. We could grow more crops.

B: What would you do with all the animals? You couldn't just let them go. Besides, some people would still hunt them. Meat has become an integral part of our diet.

A: We could provide them with better conditions anyway. We should certainly try to improve the conditions at zoos. We should try to recreate the natural conditions as much as possible.

B: That's true. I think zoo is a good idea, because they allow people to get close to animals. I think it's good for kids to see wild animals.

A: I agree. I'm an adult and I love going to the zoo. I don't like animals experiments though. I believe that we can do tests in other ways.

B: I read that the number of animals being used in experiments is falling dramatically as new techniques are being introduced.

A: That's a good news. The good thing is that most people treat their pets well.

B: Sometimes you read about people who have been cruel to pets or other animals, but those stories are rare.

A: Have you ever given money to any of the charities that take care of animals.

B: Yes, I have. They do an excellent job.

A: 你认为人们对待和利用动物的方法怎么样?

B: 大部分人都很友善地对待动物,但是我们有时对动物也很残忍。当我们饲养动物的时候,它们的生活条件往往很差。

A: 也许我们应该停止吃动物,我们可以种更多的农作物。

B: 你对所有的动物会怎么做呢?你也不能让他们自己生活。另外,人们还是照样会猎捕它们。肉类已经成为我们生活中不可缺少的一部分。

A: 不管怎么样,我们可以为他们提供一个好的条件。当然要改变动物园的条件。应尝试创造尽可能多的自然条件。

B: 你说的没错。我觉得动物园是个不错的主意,因为那儿可以让人们近距离接触动物,我想对孩子们看野生动物是一件很好的事情。

A: 同意。我是个成年人,我愿意去动物园,但是我反对对动物进行实验,我相信可以用其他的方式来做实验。

B: 我读到随着新技术的开发，被用来做实验的动物的数量正在急剧下降。

A: 这真是一个好消息，好的方面就是大部分人能很好地对待动物了。

B: 有时你也会读到那些对宠物或其他动物残忍的人们，但是这样事情很少发生。

A: 你有没有捐一些钱到慈善协会，用来保护动物们？

B: 是的，我有。他们做得非常好。

口语拓展

In the past, there have been many endangered animals. Now they are extinct. Does it matter? Has our environment been affected by their absence? Has the quality of our own life been changed? The answer to these questions is "Yes." It does matter if we destroy an endangered species habitat to develop more farmland, housing or industrial parks. There is a delicate balance of nature. If one small part is removed, it will affect all the other parts. For example, if certain trees are cut down, bats will have no place to roost. If they cannot roost, they cannot breed. If there are no bats, there will be no animal, or bird to eat certain insects that plague our crops. Our environment has been affected by the absence of certain animals.

在过去的日子里，有许多濒临绝种的动物。现在他们已经灭绝了。这要不要紧呢？他们的绝种影响到我们的环境了吗？我们的生活质量改变了吗？这些问题的答案是"是"。如果我们摧毁濒危物种栖息地而用来开发更多耕地、住宅和工业园区，这都是非常要紧的事。自然界有一种微妙的平衡。如果一小部分被移除，它将影响到所有的其他部分。例如，如果一定量的树木被砍掉，蝙蝠会没有地方栖息。如果他们不能栖息，它们无法繁殖。如果没有蝙蝠，将不会有其他动物或鸟去吃昆虫，而这些昆虫就会去危害我们的庄稼。我们的环境已经受到了一部分缺失的动物的影响。

你最好掌握的

1 integral /ˈintigrəl/ *a*. 不可或缺的，完整的，完备的

2 dramatically /drəˈmætikəli/ *ad*. 戏剧性地，引人注目地，显著地

3 charity /ˈtʃæriti/ *n*. 慈爱，仁慈；慈善团体；宽容

4 recreate /ˈriːkriˈeit/ *v*. 重新创造；娱乐；使恢复

5 endangered animal 濒危动物

6 species /ˈspiːʃiz/ *n*. 物种，种类

7 habitat /ˈhæbitæt/ *n*.（动植物的）产地、栖息地

8 roost /ruːst/ *v*. 栖息 *n*. 栖息处

9 plague /pleig/ *v*. 使……染上瘟疫；折磨 *n*. 瘟疫，灾害

Lesson

8

Trading standards

贸易标准

当前，是各国管理条例上的差异，而不是关税阻碍了发达国家之间的贸易。

虽然谈判代表持乐观态度，但协议细节如此复杂，他们所面临的困难很可能使他们根本无法取得一致。

欧洲人遵循优良的大陆传统，则希望就普遍的原则取得一致，而这些原则适用于许多不同的产品，同时可能延伸到其他国家。

你一定熟读的

情景模拟对话一

A: Good morning. Nice talking to you again. So, what can I do for you?

B: I need a couple of your SB2000 speedboats to rent to guests. Can you give me a price quote?

A: Let's see... Uh, the list price is $6, 500. You're a valued customer, so I'll give you a 10% discount.

B: That's very reasonable. Do you have them in stock?

A: Sure do! We set up new inventory controls last year, so we don't have many backlogs any more.

B: That's good. The tourist season is just around the corner, so I need them pretty quick. What's the earliest shipping date you can manage?

A: They can be ready for shipment in 2-3 weeks.

B: Perfect. What's the total CIF price?

A: Hang on... The price will be $15,230 to your usual port. Do we have a deal?

B: You bet! Send me a fax with all the information, and I'll send you my order right away. I'll pay by irrevocable letter of credit, as usual. Same terms as always?

A: Of course.

B: Great! Nice doing business with you again. Bye for now.

A: Will do, and the same goes for me. Bye.

A: 早上好，很高兴又和你谈话。我能为你做什么吗？

B: 我需要两艘你们生产的 SB2000 快艇租给游客。你能给我个报价吗？

A: 让我想想……呃，报价单上是 6500 美元。您是我们的一个重要客户，我会给您 10% 的折扣。

B: 那很合理。你们有现货吗？

A: 当然有！我们去年建立了新的存货控制系统，所以我们不再有很多的积压订单。

B: 那很好。旅游旺季就要到了，所以我很快就需要它们。您最早的发货日期是什么时候？

A: 可以在 2～3 周内准备好装船。

B: 棒极了。到岸价格是多少？

A: 稍等……价格是 15230 美元，到原先的港口。成交吗？

B: 当然！给我发一份所有相关信息的传真，我会立即下订单。我会按惯例以不可撤销信用证方式付款。按照一贯的条款吗？

A: 当然。

B: 好极了！很高兴再次和你做生意。那再见了。

A: 我会的，同样带上我的祝福。再见。

情景模拟对话二

A: Tell your graphic artists to go back to the drawing board for our new logo design. I just saw the prototype that came out of your department last week. It just won't work.

B: Why? What's the problem?

A: It is way too similar to the Nike swoosh. Don't you know? That's copyrighted. If we come out with something even close to the design they have, we could be legally liable. They'd sue us in a heartbeat.

B: I saw the design. We had a team of all-star designers on it. I don't think it resembled Nike's logo at all. That's a huge stretch of the imagination to say our design would violate their copyright.

A: Our legal department doesn't think so. They reviewed the copyrighted images from Nike. After discussion with our general manager, they determined it would be copyright infringement to place this design on our products. It's better to be safe than sorry.

B: What if we modified the design a little bit. Say we change the color. Do you think that would be enough to differentiate from the copyrighted image?

A: Nope. The verdict from the legal department is to start from scratch. This time come up with something more creative.

B: More creative?

A: Not only do we have to worry about not overstepping bounds with copyright, but we also want something different from everyone else. We want to stand out to our consumers. Come up with something good, and then we'll set our own copyright on it.

B: Okay. Looks like it's back to square one.

A: 去告诉你们的设计师回画室讨论一下我们新徽标的设计问题。我刚刚看过你们部门上星期拿出的设计样，根本不能用。

B: 为什么？有什么问题？

A: 这个设计与耐克产品上的图案太相似了。你难道不知道，这是受版权保护的？哪怕我们设计出来的东西与他们的图案接近，我们也会负法律责任的，他们会立即起诉我们。

B: 我看过那个设计，那是我们明星团队一手设计的，我认为根本不像耐克的标识。说我们的设计会侵犯他们的版权，这想象力未免有点儿太丰富了。

A: 我们的法律部门可不这么认为。他们仔细看了耐克受版权保护的图案，并和我们总经理讨论过。最后他们认定如果把这个图案放在我们的产品上，那会侵犯他们的版权。我们最好还是防患于未然吧。

B: 如果我们再修改一下设计怎么样？比如说变变颜色，你认为这样就足以与受版权保护的图案区分了吧？

A: 不行。法律部门的定论是一切从零开始。这一次要搞出更有独创性的设计。

B: 更有独创性？

A: 我们不但要小心别越过版权的权限，而且还要拿出完全与众不同的设计。我们的设计要醒目以吸引顾客。有了好的设计，我们就可以申请自己的版权了。

B: 好的。看来还是重新设计吧。

你最好掌握的

1 quote /kwəut/ *v.* 引用；报价；举例说明

2 discount /ˈdiskaunt/ *v.* 折扣；不考虑；认为……不重要 *n.* 数目，折扣

3 reasonable /ˈriːznəbl/ *a.* 通情达理的，合理的，公道的，适度的

4 in stock 库存

5 CIF price 到岸价格，成本、运费加保险费

6 graphic artist 平面设计师

7 prototype /ˈprəutətaip/ *n.* 原型

8 copyright /ˈkɔpirait/ *n.* 版权

9 liable /ˈlaiəbl/ *a.* 有义务的，有责任的，有……倾向的

10 sue /sjuː, suː/ v. 控告，请求，起诉

11 resemble /riˈzembl/ v. 相似，类似，看起来像

12 violate /ˈvaiəleit/ v. 违反，触犯，干扰

13 stretch /stretʃ/ v. 拉长，伸出，伸长，延伸 n. 伸展，延伸，延续；一段时间、路程等

14 infringement /inˈfrindʒmənt/ n. 违反，侵犯

15 modify /ˈmɔdifai/ v. 修改，更正，修饰

16 differentiate /ˌdifəˈrenʃieit/ v. 区别，差别

17 verdict /ˈvəːdikt/ n. 裁决，裁定；决定，意见

18 start from scratch 从头开始

19 be back to square one 回到原来的起点

Lesson

9

Royal espionage

你必须背诵的

王室谍报活动

阿尔弗雷德大帝曾经亲自充当间谍，他扮作吟游歌手到丹麦军队的营地里侦查。

阿尔弗雷德断定，丹麦人已不再适应持久的战争，他们的军需供应处于无组织状态，只是靠临时抢夺来维持。

他的部队不停地移动，牵着敌人的鼻子，让他们跟着他跑。

你一定熟读的

情景模拟对话一

A: Are you watching another news report about the war?

B: Yes. The two sides declared a short ceasefire but it broke down earlier today. Several military targets were destroyed by bombing. Many civilians were among the dead and wounded.

A: How did this war start?

B: Both sides tried to build border fences and began attacking each other.

A: Politicians from both sides sound increasingly belligerent. Neither side wants to compromise.

B: Relief agencies report that many civilians are in desperate need of food and shelter. Several European countries have agreed to send aid, but they are afraid that their planes will be shot down.

A: What do you think will happen?

B: Both countries are very poor. Soon they will run out of money to finance the war. Then, perhaps, they will negotiate. The thing is to find the real problem for the war and solve that.

A: It would be much simpler if they negotiated first.

A: 你是正在看另一条关于战争的报道吗?

B: 嗯，双方宣布停火，但是今天早些时候战争就陷入瘫痪中。一些军事目标已经被炸弹摧毁。很多老百姓有死亡或受伤的。

A: 这场战争是怎么开始的?

B: 两方都试图建立边境围栏，然后就开始袭击对方。

A: 两方的政客们听起来都很好战，没有一方要求妥协。

B: 救援机构报道说有很多百姓都迫切需要食物和避难所。一些欧洲国家同意提出帮助，但是都害怕他们的计划会被否决。

A: 你觉得之后会发生什么?

B: 两国都很贫穷，他们很快就会用尽支援这场战争的资金，接着可能他们就会谈判。重要的是找到问题的关键然后解决它。

A: 如果他们早就协商的话，问题就会变得简单。

情景模拟对话二

A: What do you think the main causes of war today?

B: I'd say the main reason is poverty. Countries and their people get frustrated because they have so little. If their neighbors have some resources, they try to steal them by military force.

A: It seems that a lot of wars nowadays are really civil wars. People from different ethnic groups in the same country sometimes fight for power in that country.

B: Several of those civil wars have been going on for years and years. It seems they will never end.

A: How do you think they could be ended?

B: I don't think that there is any easy way. The United Nations could send peacekeepers into the country. At least then the warring parties could be forced to negotiate.

A: So, if the cause is poverty, there should be a programme to make the country richer. If the problem is resources, share them.

B: It sounds easy when you say it like that. In reality, it's harder to make peace between countries.

A: Yes, it is. One way to stop countries fighting is to cut off their financial support. Wars are very expensive.

B: The problem is that many poor people might suffer.

A: 你觉得今天战争的主要原因是什么？

B: 我想说主要原因就是贫困。国家和人们因为钱少而很失望。如果他们的邻国有一些资源的话，他们试图通过军事力量来进行偷窃。

A: 看起来当今大部分的战争都是国内战争。同一个国家不同的种族之间有时也为了权力而打仗。

B: 这些内战每天都在持续，看起来他们永远都不会结束。

A: 你觉得他们会怎么样结束呢？

B: 我觉得没有一个好的方法。联合国可以派遣维和部队，至少交战的双方能够被迫谈判。

A: 所以，如果原因是贫困的话，也应该有一项能够使国家富裕的方案。如果问题是资源，那就与他们分享。

B: 你说的倒是容易。事实上，使两国和平是很难的一件事。

A: 也是。一个能停止战争的方法是切断他们的财政支持。战争会花费很多钱财的。

B: 问题是很多贫困的人很可能会遭殃。

你最好掌握的

1 declare /diˈklɛə/ v. 申报，宣布，声明

2 ceasefire /siːsˈfaiə/ n. 停火，停战

3 military /ˈmilitəri/ a. 军事的

4 target /ˈtɑːgit/ n. 靶；目标

5 belligerent /biˈlidʒərənt/ a. 好战的，交战的

6 compromise /ˈkɔmprəmaiz/ v. 妥协，让步

7 negotiate /niˈgəuʃieit/ v. 商议，谈判，交涉

8 agency /ˈeidʒənsi/ n. 代理，代理处

9 poverty /ˈpɔvəti/ n. 贫困，贫穷

10 frustrate /frʌsˈtreit/ v. 挫败，击败

11 ethnic /ˈeθnik/ a. 民族的，种族的

12 peacekeeper /ˈpiːsˌkiːpə(r)/ n. 维和人员

Lesson 10

Silicon valley

 你必须背诵的

硅 谷

现在有些计算机工作站使工程技术人员可以在他们的办公桌上设计、试验和生产芯片，就像一位编辑在苹果机上编出一份时事通讯一样。

作为新崛起的一代的带头人，亚裔发明家可以凭借他们在习惯和语言上的优势，与关键的太平洋沿岸市场建立起更加牢固的联系。

在硅谷变成一个退休村之前，它很可能成为建立全球商业的一个教学场地。

 你一定熟读的

情景模拟对话一

A: Would you like to purchase a computer? A desktop or notebook?

B: Notebook. Which brand do you sell?

A: We're selling HP computers. What are you looking to pay?

B: Six to seven thousand Yuan.

A: OK，take a look at this one，dual core CPU，120G hard disk and 1 GB RAM. It's 6,500 yuan. Would you like to purchase it now?

B: Thanks, but I need to think it over.

A: 要买电脑吗? 台式还是笔记本?

B: 笔记本。你这边卖什么牌子的?

A: 我们卖的是惠普的。您大概想要什么价位的?

B: 六七千元的吧。

A: 好的，您看一下这款，CPU 双核，硬盘 120G，内存 1G，才 6500 元。您现在买吗?

B: 我再考虑一下，谢谢。

情景模拟对话二

A: Hi! Is that the new laptop you bought last week? It looks very nice.

B: Yes, it is. Thanks. I'm just surfing on the internet.

A: Here? In this café? How can you do that?

B: This café offers a wireless internet connection. That means I can get on the net for free while I'm here. Of course, I have to buy a cup of coffee!

A: That's great. Can you do it anywhere?

B: No, you can only do it when the café offers a wireless connection. There are only about 10 or 12 places that offer it in this city.

A: So, what programs do you have on your laptop?

B: I've got all the usual ones for word processing and then I have a few for creating and editing photographs.

A: I know you are keen on photography. It's very useful for you to be able to download photos from your digital camera. Then you attach the picture files to emails and send them to anyone, anywhere, at anytime!

B: It's wonderful, isn't it? Would you like to see some photos that I took recently?

A: Of course I would like to.

A: 嗨，这是你上个星期买的新的笔记本电脑吗？它很漂亮呀。

B: 嗯，谢谢，我刚刚在网上冲浪呢。

A: 这儿吗？这家咖啡店？你怎么做到的？

B: 这个咖啡店提供无线上网连接，也就是说我只要在这儿，我就能免费上网。当然，你必须得买一杯咖啡。

A: 真是太棒了，这个哪儿都能上网吗？

B: 不是，你只能在咖啡店提供的无线上网连接才可以，这个城市也只有10家或12家地方能提供这样条件的。

A: 你的电脑都有什么程序？

B: 我刚刚安装了一些常用的文字程序，我也有一些制作和修改图片的程序。

A: 我知道你钟爱摄影，这对你能从数码相机上下载图片是很有帮助的。然后你就可以把图片文件贴到邮箱，然后随时发到你想发的任何一个地方，任何一个人那里，想发的地方了。

B: 这不是很好吗？你想不想看看我最近拍的照片？

A: 我当然愿意。

 你最好掌握的

1 purchase /'pɜːtʃəs/ v. 购买

2 laptop /'læptɒp/ n. 便携式电脑

3 surfing on the internet 网上冲浪

4 wireless /'waɪəlɪs/ a. 无线的

5 digital /'dɪdʒɪtl/ a. 数字的

Lesson

11

How to grow old

 你必须背诵的

如何安度晚年

个人的存在应该像一条河流，开始很小，被紧紧地夹在两岸中间，接着热情奔放地冲过巨石，飞下瀑布。

克服死的最好办法——至少在我看来是这样——就是逐渐使自己的兴趣更加广泛，逐渐摆脱个人狭小的圈子，直到自我的围墙一点一点地倒塌下来，自己的生活慢慢地和整个宇宙的生活融合一起。

随着精力的衰退，老年人的疲惫感会增长，有长眠的愿望未尝不是一件好事。

 你一定熟读的

情景模拟对话

A: How many people are in your family?

B: As you know, China has a single-child policy. Therefore, there's just my husband, my daughter and I. What about in your family?

A: I have one daughter and one son. Then there's my husband and I. What about your parents? Do they live with your family?

B: Not anymore. They live with my brother now, what about you?

A: My parents live by themselves now. When they get older, they'll probably go to a retirement home. Do you just have one brother?

B: No, I have two older brothers and one younger sister. What about you?

A: I also grew up in a big family. I have one older brother and three younger sisters.

B: How long have you been married?

A: About seven years now, and you?

B: I've been married for about five years. What do you think about divorce?

A: It's becoming more and more common. However, I don't ever want to get divorced myself! What about you?

B: If my husband cheated on me or treated me badly, I would get a divorce.

A: If that happens, maybe you could marry my brother and we could become in-laws!

B: (ha ha) I'll keep that in mind, but don't tell my husband.

A: Of course not!

A: 你们家有几口人?

B: 你知道的,中国有独生子女政策。所以,只有我的丈夫,我和我的女儿。你家呢?

A: 我有一个女儿和一个儿子。此外,还有我的丈夫和我,你的父母怎么样?他们是否与你一起生活?

B: 没有了。他们与我的哥哥一起生活了。你们呢?

A: 我的父母自己住了。他们老了,可能会去一个养老院。你只有一个兄弟?

B: 不,我有两个哥哥,一个妹妹。你呢?

A: 我也生长在一个大家庭。我有一个哥哥,三个妹妹。

B: 你结婚多长时间了?

A: 到现在已经七年了,你呢?

B: 我已经五年了,你怎么看离婚?

A: 这已经成为越来越普遍的现象了。不过，我从来没有想过离婚！你呢？

B: 如果我的丈夫欺骗了我，或待我不好，我就会想离婚。

A: 如果发生这种情况，也许你能嫁给我的兄弟，我们可以成为亲家了！

B:（哈哈）我会记住的，但不要告诉我的丈夫。

A: 当然不会了。

口语拓展

As the result of birth control and improvement of medical care, supporting the old has become an issue of China today.

Because of the different culture and tradition, supporting the old is different from country to country. For instance, Britain is a developed country and the problem of supporting the old is solved very well these years. The government takes a series of measures to solve the problem and also pays a lot of money for the old every year in order to make them live better.

In China, because of its tradition, the old people are mostly supported by their children. But our government and our society are taking measures to support the old.

作为计划生育和医疗改革的结果，赡养老人已成为今日中国的一个问题。

因为不同的文化和传统，赡养老人的问题各国各不相同。例如，英国是一个发达国家，赡养老人的问题，这些年一直解决得很好。政府采取一系列措施来解决这个问题，并且每年都花费大量资金以使老人们生活得更好。

在中国，因为传统的原因，老人总是由子女赡养。但是我们的政府和社会都在采取措施，来解决赡养老人这一问题。

你最好掌握的

1 retirement /ri'taiəmənt/ *n*. 退休

2 divorce /di'vɔːs/ *n*. 离婚 *v*. 与……办离婚

3 cheat /tʃiːt/ *v*. 欺骗；作弊 *n*. 骗子，欺骗行为

4 in-laws 姻亲（无血缘关系的亲戚）

5 improvement /im'pruːvmənt/ *n*. 改进，改良

6 issue /'isjuː/ *n*. 问题；发行物；发出，发行；一期，期号 *v*. 出版，发行，发表，发布，宣布，将……诉诸法律；冒出，流出；传出

7 tradition /trə'diʃən/ *n*. 传统，惯例

8 solve /sɒlv/ *v*. 解答（难题），解决

9 a series of 一系列

Lesson

12　Banks and their customers

银行和顾客

任何人在银行开一个活期账户，就等于把钱借给了银行。这笔钱他可以随时提取，提取的方式可以是取现金，也可以是开一张以他人为收款人的支票。

银行必须遵照储户的嘱托办事，不能听从其他人的指令。

储户首次在银行开户的时候，嘱咐银行他的存款只能凭他本人签字的支票来提取。

你一定熟读的

情景模拟对话一

A: Excuse me, I want to deposit some money in my account, but I don't know how to do it.

B: OK, let me help you. Please hand me your money.

A: All right, here you are, not a big sum.

B: I will deposit the sum in your account, please wait for a moment.

A: Okay, is there anything else I should do?

B: No, just wait please. All right, the sum has been put into your account. Take this receipt which has all of the transaction information on it.

A: Thanks a lot. I really appreciate it.

A: 你好，我想往账户里存点儿钱，可不知道怎么存。

B: 好的，我来，钱先给我。

A: 好的，给，没多少钱。

B: 我会把钱存进您的账户，请稍等。

A: 好，还有什么其他手续吗？

B: 没了，您稍等就行。好了，钱已经存进去了。这是存款凭证，上面有这笔存款的相关信息。

A: 谢谢，太谢谢了。

情景模拟对话二

A: Good morning, sir. I am from Japan. My English is poor. Can you help me?

B: It is my pleasure，but I think it would be better for you to tell me what you want to do.

A: Oh，I want to change some money, but I do not know how to fill out the exchange memo.

B: Would you care to give me your passport and write your name on the paper?

A: Here you are. My name is Tanaka.

B: Good. I will fill out the exchange memo for you now. Why do not you take a seat over there for a moment?

A: I would like to. Thanks.

B: Hello, Mr. Tanaka. I was wondering if you would ever thought of conversing the unused Renminbi back into Japan yen later?

A: Yes, if I will have Renminbi left.

B: So, if I may make a suggestion, please keep your exchange memo safe.

A: Thank you indeed. I will do that.

B: Not at all.

A: 你好，先生。我是日本人。我的英语不太好，你能帮忙吗？

B: 很高兴为您效劳，但我想您最好告诉我您想要干什么。

A: 啊，我想兑换些钱，但不知道怎样填写兑换水单。我不会看英文。

B: 您能把您的护照给我，并把您的名字写在这张纸上吗？

A: 给你护照和姓名，我叫田中。

B: 好，我现在就为您填写这张兑换水单。您请在那里坐一会行吗？

A: 好的，谢谢。

B: 您好，田中先生，不知道您是否考虑到以后要把没有用完的人民币兑换成日元呢？

A: 是的，如果有没用完的人民币的话，就要换成日元。

B: 那么，如果我还可以提一个建议的话，请您保管好您的这张兑换水单。

A: 我会保管好的。谢谢。

B: 不用谢。

你最好掌握的

1 account /ə'kaunt/ *n*. 账目，报告，账户；描述，记述 *v*. 叙述，解释

2 sum /sʌm/ *n*. 总数，全部，金额 *v*. 合计，总结

3 receipt /ri'si:t/ *n*. 收据

4 transaction /træn'zækʃən/ *n*. 交易，处理，办理

5 appreciate /ə'pri:ʃieit/ *v*. 欣赏，感激，赏识；领会，意识；使增值，涨价

6 fill out 填写（表格）

7 memo /'meməu/ *n*. 备忘录

8 wonder /'wʌndə/ *n*. 奇迹，惊奇，惊叹，惊诧 *v*. 惊奇，想知道，怀疑

9 indeed /in'di:d/ *ad*. 的确，真正地

Lesson 13

The search for oil

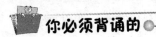
探寻石油

我是专门搞石油的，寻找石油比其他任何采矿活动对改进深孔钻探作的贡献都要大。

这种钻头能切割一段光滑的圆柱形岩石，从中能看出钻头所钻透的地层。

我们尽量避免使用过时的不实用的喷井方法，那样会浪费石油和天然气。

你一定熟读的

情景模拟对话一

A: Does your country export a lot of natural resources?

B: We export some coal to European countries, but our biggest exports is copper, which we export to Europe, North America, and China.

A: Which resources do you have to import?

B: We import a little oil from Venezuela, but we are fairly self-sufficient. We import some iron and a lot of aluminium from neighouring countries.

A: I heard that your country recently discovered deposits of precious stone.

B: Yes, that's right. So far, only small deposits have been found. Engineers in my country are focusing on drilling for oil. The government is keen to exploit our natural resources to get money to export other's countries.

A: If your government invests in your country's infrastructure, the money will spend by the very values.

B: Yes. We need to put the money into long-term projects rather than wasting it on short-term ones.

A: 贵国是否出口大量的自然资源？

B: 我们出口煤炭到欧洲一些国家，但我们最大的出口是铜，我们出口铜到欧洲、北美和中国。

A: 哪些资源你们必须进口？

B: 我们从委内瑞拉进口一点石油，但我们可以基本上自给自足。我们从邻国进口的钢铁和铝很多。

A: 我听说你们国家最近发现宝石。

B: 是的，没错。到目前为止，只有一小部分矿产已被发现。我国的工程重点是进行石油钻探。政府热衷于利用我们的自然资源利用出口到其他国家得到资金。

A: 如果贵国政府投资基础设施，这钱会花得值。

B: 是。我们需要投入的是长期项目，而不是在短期浪费这笔钱。

情景模拟对话二

A: Is there a lot of oil and coal in your country?

B: There is some, but my country is not amongst the leading producers. The oil and coal deposits are in the north of my country. Your country is a big oil producer, isn't it?

A: Yes, it is. My country is famous for having that natural resources. We also have a lot of natural gas.

B: We have some too. Do you have a lot of coal?

A: No coal has been discovered in my country, but there may be undiscovered deposits. We don't have many metal deposits.

B: There are a few in my country. We have deposit of gold, but they are very small.

A: When I traveled around your country, I bought some jewellery made from gold form your country. The jewellery told me that there are few gold mines in your country. The gold was found in mountain.

B: That's right. A few people go panning for gold in rivers.

A: You have many trees in your country. That's another natural resources.

B: It's a natural resources that we hardly use. Government policy is to conserve those forests.

A: I see. That's probably a good idea. Too many forest are being destroyed.

B: Is your country's environment being damaged by the oil industry?

A: It is very hard to avoid pollution when extracting oil. There has been some damage, but it is under control.

A: 贵国是否有许多石油和煤炭?

B: 有一些,但我国并没有跻身在龙头企业中去。石油和煤炭储量在我国北方。贵国是一个大产油国,是不是?

A: 是的。我国是以自然资源而闻名。我们也有大量的天然气。

B: 我们也有一些。你们有很多的煤?

A: 煤炭一直没有被我们国家发现,但可能会有未发现的矿。我们没有很多金属矿。

B: 目前我国只有少数。我们有金矿,但它们都很小。

A: 我去贵国旅游,我买了一些贵国制造的黄金首饰。首饰商告诉我,在您的国家金矿很少。黄金都在山区被发现的。

B: 对。一些人去河流淘黄金。

A: 贵国有很多树木。这是另一种自然资源。

B: 这是一个我们几乎不使用自然资源。政府的政策是要保护这些森林。

A: 我明白了。这可能是个好主意。太多的森林正在被摧毁。

B: 贵国的环境正在被石油工业所破坏吗?

A: 很难在提取石油时避免污染,会有一些损害,但是在控制之中。

你最好掌握的

1 copper /'kɔpə/ a.(紫)铜色的,铜(制)的 n. 铜,铜币,铜制品

2 self-sufficient /'selfsə'fʃənt/ a. 自给自足的

3 focus /'fəukəs/ n. 焦点,焦距 v. 集中,聚集,使集中

4 drill /dril/ v. 训练,钻孔 n. 钻孔机,钻床;训练,练习

5 infrastructure /'infrə'strʌktʃə/ n. 下部构造,基础结构,基础设施

6 long-term /'lɔːŋ'təm/ a. 长期的

7 exploit /iks'plɔit/ v. 开发,利用,开采,发挥

8 amongst /ə'mʌŋst/ prep. 在……之中,在……之间

9 deposit /di'pɔzit/ n. 存款,订金,堆积物,保证金;矿床,矿藏

10 policy /'pɔlisi/ n. 政策,方针

11 conserve /kən'səːv/ v. 保护,保藏,保存;节约,节省 n. 蜜饯,果酱

12 extract /iks'trækt/ v. 摘录,提取,吸取,拔出 n. 摘录,引用;选录;提炼物,浓缩物

Lesson

14

The Butterfly Effect

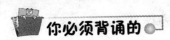

你必须背诵的

蝴蝶效应

世界上最好的两三天以上的天气预报具有很强的推测性，如果超过六七天，天气预报就没有了任何价值。

错误和不可靠性上升，接踵而来的是一系列湍流的征兆，从小尘暴和暴风发展到只有卫星上可以看到的席卷整块大陆的漩涡。

即使是这样，有些开始时的资料也不得不依靠推测，因为地面工作站和卫星不可能看到地球上的每一个地方。

 你一定熟读的

情景模拟对话一

A: What are you doing?

B: I'm just looking at this map of the world. I'm preparing for a geography class.

A: There are no countries marked on the map.

B: No, there aren't. This map just show the geographical features. Look, the Himalayan plateau with the highest peaks in the world.

A: The thing that I find most surprising is that most of the world is covered with water. Compared to the oceans, most countries are tiny.

B: I find it incredible how millions of years of volcanic activity have created mountains thousands of metres high.

A: Rivers have created deep valleys and canyons like the Grand Canyou.

B: The oceans and landscapes all influence our climate.

A: It's all so interesting. I'll have to find more information about it on the internet. Or perhaps I should try and attend your geography class.

A: 你在干什么呢?

B: 我只是看看这张世界地图。我正在准备地理课。

A: 这个地图没有标志国家。

B: 是没有。这个地图只显示相关的地理特征。看,世界的最高峰喜马拉雅山峰。

A: 我觉得最惊讶的是,世界上大多数是被水覆盖。相对于海洋,大多数国家都小。

B: 我觉得难以置信的是,几百万年的火山活动创造了数千米高的山脉。

A: 河流所创造的深邃的山谷,像科罗拉多大峡谷。

B: 海洋和地貌都影响我们的气候。

A: 真有趣。我必须在互联网上找到它更多的信息。也许我应该试试加入到你们的地理课。

情景模拟对话二

A: What's the weather like in your city?

B: In the summer it gets very hot. The temperture is often between 37 and 40 centigrade. When it is hot we often get rains, the winters are drier.

A: The summer tempreture often reaches about 20 to 25 in my city, the rain falls mostly in the winter, and we often get snow.

B: What are the temperatures in winter? In my city it is about 15 to 20 degrees.

A: In winter temperture often falls to zero, at night temperture can be below that, the streets are often icing in the morning. With such tempertures, it must has some thunderstorms.

B: Yeah, we do. In the middle of summer there can be found storms every day ususally in the afternoon. I heard your city has a lot of fog, is that true?

A: We do have a few fog days in winter, but I would not say we have a lot of fogs. The sky are usually clearly in your city, are they?

B: Yes, they are. Like I said we have thunderstorms, but each one usually last a few hours, then the sky is clear again.

A: Have you ever had snow in your city?

B: My grandmother said there was snow once when she was a child, but my parents and I never see it in my city.

A: The river in my city sometime freeze over, people go ice-skating on it. In summer people go boating on the river, but few people go swimming because it is not very clean.

B: As you know, my city is on the coast. The water is also not clean, but people still go swimming all year around. I perfer to sand bath on the beach when the weather is hot.

A: 你们城市的天气怎么样?

B: 夏天非常热。温度经常是37～40℃。当天气热的时候,这儿又常常会下雨,冬天变得却更干燥。

A: 夏季在我们这气温往往维持在20～25℃之间,降雨主要集中在冬季,我们这经常下雪。

B: 冬天是什么温度? 在我们这是大约15～20℃。

A: 在冬季气温往往下降到零度,夜间温度低于零度,可以说,街上经常在早上结冰。这样的温度下一定会有一些雷暴雨。

B: 是的。在夏季中部每天经常下午还会下暴雨。我听说你们城市有很多的雾,是真的吗?

A: 我们确实在冬季有一些大雾天,但我不认为我们有很多雾。

在你们城市天空是很晴朗的，是吗？

B: 是的。就像我说我们有雷暴雨，但每一次通常持续几个小时，然后天空就会放晴了。

A: 你们那里下过雪吗？

B: 我的祖母说，当她还是个孩子时下过一次雪，但我的父母和我从来没有看到。

A: 在我这儿河流有时会冻结，人们就会到上面溜冰。在夏天，人们在河里划船，但是很少人去游泳，因为它不是很干净。

B: 你知道的，我们这靠着海岸。水也不是很干净的，但人们仍然每年都去游泳。我更喜欢在天气炎热的时候晒沙滩浴。

 你最好掌握的

1 feature /ˈfiːtʃə/ n. 面貌，特色，特性，特写
2 Himalayan plateau 喜马拉雅山峰
3 peak /piːk/ n. 山顶，顶点
4 compare to 与……相比
5 volcanic /vɔlˈkænik/ a. 火山的
6 incredible /inˈkredəbl/ a. 难以置信的
7 landscape /ˈlændskeip/ n. 风景，山水，风景画
8 influence /ˈinfluəns/ n. 影响力，感化力；势力，权势 v. 影响，感化
9 thunderstorm /ˈθʌndəstɔːm/ n. 雷暴雨（大雷雨）
10 fog /fɔg/ n. 雾 v. 以雾笼罩，被雾笼罩

Lesson

15

Secrecy in industry

你必须背诵的

工业中的秘密

有两个因素严重地妨碍着工业中科学研究的效率：一是科研工作中普遍存在的保密氛围；二是研究人员缺乏个人自由。

然而，依赖这种研究的很多工艺程序是在完全保密的情况下进行的，直到可以取得专利权的阶段为止。

很多公司向图书馆借阅科技书籍时感到很困难，因为它们不愿让人家记下来它们公司的名字和借阅的某一图书。

你一定熟读的

情景模拟对话一

A: Nice to meet you, Mr. Kim. I am honored to have the opportunity to attend this meeting.

B: Me too. Mr. Jim. We will take this opportunity to exchange opinions and make future plans.

A: Okay, let's cut to the chase. My report is divided into 3 parts which will be demonstrated on the screen.

B: My group will present the financial analysis report and the prospect estimation.

A: I hope our coordination can push this plan forward and that we can achieve success together.

B: I believe we will. Let's get started.

A: 很高兴见到您，金先生。很荣幸有机会出席这次会议。

B: 我也是。吉姆先生。我们借此机会正好交换一下意见，然后制订一下前景规划。

A: 好，我们直入主题吧。我的报告分为三部分，分别会在屏幕上演示。

B: 我们组会向各位作财务分析报告和前景预期判断。

A: 希望我们的合作可以推动计划进行并最终取得成功。

B: 我深信此点。我们开始吧。

情景模拟对话二

A: What do you think we need to do to get our new branch office running well?

B: First，I'd make sure that we have a good local corporate lawyer. He or she will know all the local laws and regulations.

A: That's very important. A friend recommended a good law firm to me. We'll need someone to hire staff.

B: I think that we should send one of our HR people to do that. I don't think we should use an agency，because they won't be familiar with the type of people we employ. Have we decide on the location of the branch office?

A: Yes，we have. We chose the location in the northeast of the city, not too far from the airport and on the edge of the CBD.

B: Why didn't we choose an office in the CBD?

A: The offices there were too expensive. Have we negotiated any contracts?

B: Yes. We've signed two contracts with companies. We hope to sign another three this month.

A: When will the branch office open?

B: Hopefully next month. Everything is a little rushed. We should be able to set up our branch office and expand our business quickly.

A: Has the advertising campaign been prepared?

B: Yes, it has. We're going to target the business community through business magazine.

A: I made plenty of business contract on my last visit and through the embassy. We should be able to get plenty of customers.

A: 你认为要让我们的分支机构办好需要做什么?

B: 首先,我会确保我们有一个好的,当地的企业律师。他或她知道所有的地方性法规和规章。

A: 这是非常重要的。一个朋友向我推荐一个好的律师事务所。我们将需要有人去雇用工作人员。

B: 我认为我们应该派人力资源部的一个人去做。我认为我们不应该使用代理,因为他们不熟悉我们雇用的人。我们已经决定分支办公室的位置了吗?

A: 是。我们选择了在城市的东北位置,离机场以及商务中心区都不远。

B: 为什么我们不在商务中心找一个办公室呢?

A: 那儿的办公室租金太昂贵了。我们有谈判的任何合同吗?

B: 是。我们已经签署了两个公司。希望这个月签署其他三个合同。

A: 分支机构什么时候开?

B: 希望下个月。一切都有点匆忙。我们应该迅速建立我们的分公司和扩大我们的业务。

A: 广告运作准备得怎么样了?

B: 是的,都准备好了。我们将通过商业杂志锁定商界为目标。

A: 我在上次访问中通过使馆签了大量的商业合同,我们应该能够获得大量的客户。

你最好掌握的

1 chase /tʃeis/ v. 追捕，追逐，追求 n. 追捕，狩猎

2 exchange /iks'tʃeindʒ/ v. 交换，交易，兑换

3 analysis /ə'næləsis/ n. 分析，解析

4 prospect /'prɔspekt/ n. 景色，希望，展望，前途 v. 探勘，寻找

5 estimation /esti'meiʃən/ n. 判断，估计

6 branch /brɑ:ntʃ/ n. 分枝，树枝

7 corporate /'kɔ:pərit/ a. 社团的，法人的，共同的

8 recommend /rekə'mend/ v. 建议，推荐，劝告，介绍

9 contract /'kɔntrækt/ n. 合同，契约 v. 染上（恶习，疾病等）；缩小；订立（婚约），订契约

10 community /kə'mju:niti/ n. 社区，团体

11 embassy /'embəsi/ n. 大使馆

Lesson

16

The modern city

 你必须背诵的

现代城市

在工业生活的组织中，工厂对工人的生理和精神状态的影响完全被忽视了。

现代工业的基本概念是：以最低成本获取最多产品，为的是让某个人或某一部分人尽可能多地赚钱。

在享受自己住宅的舒适和庸俗的豪华时，却没有意识到被剥夺了生活所必需的东西。

现代工业发展起来了，却根本没有想到操作机器的人的本质。

 你一定熟读的

情景模拟对话

A: How do you think the transport system in our city could be improved?

B: I think that the public transport system could be made simpler. I never know where the bus routes actually go. The routes seem to twist and turn rather than going roughly in a straight line.

A: I think we just need to build more roads. Then there would be more space for cars to drive and we'd have fewer traffic jams.

B: If we built more roads, people would just fill them with cars again. I think we should discourage people from using their cars.

A: How would you do that?

B: I think we should do a few things at once. Improving public transport would encourage people to use that. If we also charge people to use their cars in the city centre, they won't use their cars as much.

A: I don't know. I think it's unfair to make drivers pay more money. They already pay a lot of petrol tax, for example.

B: I think that they should pay more tax. Look at the damage they cause to the environment and people's health by discharging all those exhaust fumes.

A: The air would certainly be cleaner if there were fewer cars being used in the city. The problem is that people will see it as reducing their freedom. It well be unpopular.

B: That's a good point. Car owners will probably be against it, but people who use public transport will be in favor of it.

A: 你认为在我们的城市交通运输系统可以如何改善?

B: 我认为公共交通系统可以简化些。我从来不知道真正的巴士路线要怎么样走。这些路线似乎迂回曲折,而不是大致在一条直线上。

A: 我认为我们只需要兴建更多的道路。然后,将会有更多的空间来驾驶汽车,也会减少交通拥堵。

B: 如果我们建立更多的道路,人们将又把道路堵满汽车。我认为我们应该减少汽车的使用。

A: 你会怎么做呢?

B: 我觉得我们应该马上做一些事情。改善公共交通,鼓励人们使用它们。如果我们对在市中心使用车辆的人们收费的话,他们将尽量不使用他们的汽车了。

A: 我不知道。我认为让司机支付更多的钱是不公平的。例如,他们已经付出了很多,汽油税。

B: 我认为他们应该付出更多的税。看看他们排放废气对环境和人们健康所造成的这些损害。

A: 如果在城市使用更少的汽车，空气肯定会清洁。但问题是，人们会觉得就像减少了他们的自由一样，这也不受欢迎。

B: 说的没错。车主可能会反对，但是人们使用公共交通工具将会更受欢迎。

口语拓展

There are many reasons for the great change in the ownership of houses in cities. The development of the economy is the most important one. Thanks to this development, people make more money than they used to. As a result, they can set aside some money to buy houses after their daily necessities are satisfied. The measures the government adopts may be the next incentive. Nowadays, people can have access to various kinds of loans from banks when buying the house. Wherever you go, you can see houses of various designs and sizes available for people to choose. These changes will have a great influence on both the living standard of the individual and the productivity of the society. People can live in the spacious houses of their own and the government can increase the productivity by using the money from selling the houses.

城市房屋所有权产生巨大变化的原因有很多。经济的发展是最重要的。由于这方面的发展，人们赚的钱比以前多了。因此，他们可以留出一些钱，在满足生活日用品需要后买房子。政府采取的措施，可能成为下一个鼓励。现在，当人们买房子时可以以各种形式从银行贷款。无论你去哪里，你都可以看到各种设计和户型的房子供人们选择。这些变化将会对个人的生活水平和社会生产力有重大影响。人们能够生活在自己宽敞的房子里，政府可以用销售房子的钱来提高生产力。

你最好掌握的

1 transport /træns'pɔːt/ v. 运输；流放 n. 运输、运输工具；（常用复数）强烈的情绪

2 route /ruːt/ n. 航线，路线

3 roughly /'rʌfli/ ad. 概略地，粗糙地

4 discourage /dis'kʌridʒ/ v. 使气馁，阻碍

5 tax /tæks/ n. 税，税额 v. 向……征税；消耗精力

6 discharge /dis'tʃɑːdʒ/ v. 卸下，放出，偿还，执行 n. 释放；排除的物体

7 exhaust /ig'zɔːst/ v. 用尽，耗尽，使……精疲力尽

8 fume /fjuːm/ n. 烟雾，气味 v. 愤怒；冒烟

9 environment /in'vaiərənmənt/ n. 环境

10 ownership /'əunəʃip/ n. 所有权

11 economy /i(ː)'kɔnəmi/ n. 节约，经济

12 daily necessity 日常必需品

13 various /'vɛəriəs/ a. 各种各样的

14 influence on 对……有影响

15 productivity /ˌprɔdʌk'tiviti/ n. 生产率，生产力

16 available /ə'veiləbəl/ a. 可用的，有效的

17 access /'ækses/ n. 通道，入口，接近……的权利（方法）

18 set aside 把……放在一边；不理会；取消，驳回

Lesson

17

A man-made disease

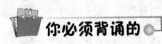 你必须背诵的

人为的疾病

这种兔子在澳大利亚及新西兰没有天敌，因此便以兔子所特有的杂乱交配迅猛繁殖起来。

后来又发现，有一种蚊子是传播这种疾病的媒介，能把此病传染给兔子。

后来明显看出，兔子对这种疾病已经产生了一定程度的免疫力，所以兔子不可能被完全消灭。

野兔在法国一般不被当作有害动物，而被视为打猎取乐的玩物和有用的食物来源。

 你一定熟读的

情景模拟对话一

A: Good morning, Mr. Morgan. How are you today?

B: A little better than yesterday.

A: Has the chest pain decreased a little?

B: Yes, it has.

A: I'm happy to hear that. Do you sleep well?

B: Just fine.

A: The doctor ordered that you should stay in bed for several days, and if you feel any shortness of breath, please let me know. I'll tell the doctor. Your diet is about low cholesterol and sodium.

B: Thank you, nurse, it isn't necessary now. I'll follow the doctor's order.

A: 您好，摩根先生，您今天怎样？

B: 比昨天稍好一点。

A: 胸痛好些了吗？

B: 是的，好些了。

A: 很高兴听到这些。那您睡得好吗？

B: 还好。

A: 医生说，您应该卧床休息些日子，如果您感到气急，请告诉我，我会转告医生的。您的饮食应低胆固醇，低钠。

B: 护士，谢谢你。现在还不需要。我将遵照医嘱去做。

情景模拟对话二

A: Doctor, would you please treat disease of my wife? She sings and dances round the clock, sometimes just like an actress, and sometimes she laughs loudly as well as cries. Maybe she is mad.

B: What else?

A: In very severe cases, she beat some persons.

B: How long has she been like this?

A: Over one week, but her condition has been getting worse to worse for a few days.

B: Now, let me give her a neurological examination. But some further examinations should be done, including an electroencephalogram and a brain scan and so on .

A: Doctor, is her disease very serious? Is it curable?

B: Yes, this case could be cured. But she may have a relapse. This is a natural phenomenon. Don't worry.

A: At what cases and when might a relapse have?

B: It is hard to say that. For it varies from individual to individual, perhaps a long or a short time. It may be a few days, or a few months. In a word, it relies on a great many factors, such as circumstances, rest, treatment and so forth. Because her condition is very serious, I suggest she should go to a psychiatric hospital to be treated. A stay in that hospital for a long period of intensive treatment may be curable.

A: Thanks a lot, doctor.

A: 医生，请您给我妻子治一治病吧！她昼夜不停地唱歌、跳舞，有时就像一个演员，有时她还大哭大笑。她可能是疯了。

B: 还有什么症状？

A: 病重时，她还要打人。

B: 她像这样有多久了？

A: 有一个多星期了，可是近几天病情越来越重。

B: 现在我全面地给她做一个神经科检查。不过还要做进一步的检查，如脑电图和脑扫描等。

A: 医生，她的病很重吗？能治好吗？

B: 是的，这种病是能治愈的，但可能会有反复。这是自然的，不要着急。

A: 什么情况下，或什么时候可能有反复呢？

B: 很难说。因为情况因人而异。有的人可能时间长，有的则可能短。也许是几天，或几个月。总之，反复和许多因素有关。如：外界环境、休息情况、治疗情况等。由于她的病很重，我建议将她转到精神病院去治疗。在那儿住上一段较长时间的医院，进行积极治疗，她的病也许会好的。

A: 十分感谢，医生。

你最好掌握的

1 decrease /diːˈkriːs/ v . 减少，缩短 n . 减少量；降低

2 chest /tʃest/ n . 胸，胸部；衣柜

3 shortness /ˈʃɔːtnis/ n . 短小，简略，不足

4 cholesterol /kəˈlestərəul,-rɔl/ n . 胆固醇

5 sodium /ˈsəudjəm,-diəm/ n . 钠

6 neurological /njuərəuˈlɔdʒikəl/ a . 神经病学的

7 scan /skæn/ v . 扫描，详细调查 n . 扫描

8 curable /ˈkjuərəb(ə)l/ a . 可医治的，医得好的

9 relapse /riˈlæps/ v . 故态复萌，再度恶化

10 phenomenon /fiˈnɔminən/ n . 现象

11 circumstance /ˈsəːkəmstəns/ n . 环境，状况，事件

12 treatment /ˈtriːtmənt/ n . 治疗

13 psychiatric /saikiˈætrik/ a . 精神病的

14 intensive /inˈtensiv/ a . 集中的，强化的，精细的，深入的

15 vary /ˈvɛəri/ v . 变化，改变，不同

Lesson

18   Porpoises

 你必须背诵的

海 豚

海洋摄影室的生物学家指出，无论海豚多么的聪明，认为它们有救人的动机可能是错误的。

海豚和鲨鱼是天然仇敌，双方可能随之发生搏斗，搏斗的结果是海豚赶走或咬死鲨鱼。

它们经常追逐海龟，海龟则温顺地忍受着各种侮辱。

小海豚特别喜欢用鼻子把海龟推到水面，然后像滑水板一样把海龟从水池的这一边推到那一边。

此时的海龟，只要能站起来就满足了，但它刚站起来，就被一只海豚击倒。

 你一定熟读的

口语拓展一

A shortage of fish and other food is threatening many of the world's penguins. As many as ten of seventeen kinds of penguins may be in danger of disappearing. Penguins are black and white birds that live in the southern half of the world. They are common to South America, New Zealand, Australia and South Africa. Many live near cold waters. But some live near warm waters in the Galapagos Islands, near the coast of Ecuador. Penguins cannot fly. But they are fine swimmers. Penguins eat fish. Some kinds of penguins eat a small shrimp — like crustacean called krill. Many scientists blame global warming for the decrease in penguin populations. They believe the heating of the atmosphere has caused ocean waters to become warmer and higher water temperatures have reduced the supply of fish and krill. Rising air and water temperatures may have especially harmed Galapagos penguins. Researchers say that some years these birds are completely unable to reproduce. In addition, many adult penguins die of hunger.

鱼和其他食物的短缺威胁着世界上的企鹅。17 种企鹅中的 10 种正面临着灭绝的危险。企鹅是一种生活在南半球的黑白相间的鸟。它们大多数生活在南美洲、新西兰、澳大利亚和南非。大部分生活在冷水域中，但也有些生活在厄瓜多尔海岸附近加拉帕哥斯群岛的温水域中。企鹅不会飞。但是它们是很好的游泳者。企鹅是吃鱼的。一些种类的企鹅吃小的虾类，如甲壳类的磷虾。大多数科学家认为全球变暖是使企鹅数量减少的主要原因，他们认为大气变暖使海水变温，高的海水温度造成鱼和磷虾的供应减少。大气和海水的温度上升对加拉帕哥斯群岛的企鹅有特别的害处。研究员们说过几年这些鸟将会完全的失去繁殖的能力。此外，许多成年企鹅死于饥饿。

口语拓展二

Animals are natural resources that people have wasted all through our history. Animals have been killed for their fur and feathers, for food, for sport, and simply because they were in the way. Thousands of kinds of animals have disappeared from the earth forever. Hundreds more are on the danger list today. About 170 kinds in the United States alone are considered in danger.

Why should people care? Because we need animals, and because once they are gone, there will never be any more. Animals are more than just beautiful or interesting. They are more than just a source of food. Every animal has its place in the balance of nature. Destroying one kind of animal can create many problems. Some people are working to help save the animals. Some groups raise money to let people know about the problem. And they try to get the governments to pass laws protecting animals in danger. Quite a few countries have passed laws. These laws forbid the killing of any animals or plants on the danger list. Widespread fishing, exploration for oil and oil leaks also threaten penguins. Poisonous organisms in ocean water are another danger.

　　动物是自然资源，在整个历史过程中，人类一直在浪费着这种资源。人们杀死动物，获得它们的皮毛，把它们当作食物或运动方式，或者只是因为它们碍事。成千上万种动物已经从这个地球上永远地消失了。现在另外上百种动物也上了濒危动物名单。仅美国大概就有170种被认为处于危险当中。

　　为什么人们应该感到担忧呢？因为我们需要动物，因为它们一旦消失，就永远不会再出现。动物不仅仅是漂亮或有趣。它们不仅仅是人类的食物来源。在维持自然平衡中，每种动物都有其作用。毁灭某种动物会导致许多问题。有些人正在努力帮助拯救这些动物。有些组织筹钱以便人们了解这一问题。他们也努力使政府通过保护濒危动物的法律。很多国家已经通过了法律。这些法律禁止杀害濒危名单上的任何动、植物。大规模捕鱼，勘探原油和石油的泄漏同样威胁着企鹅，海水中的有毒的有机物是另一个威胁。

你最好掌握的

1 penguin /'peŋgwin/ *n*. 企鹅

2 disappear /ˌdisə'piə/ *v*. 消失，不见

3 completely /kəm'pliːtli/ *ad*. 完全地，十分地

4 reproduce /ˌriːprə'djuːs/ *v*. 再生，复制，生殖

5 balance /'bæləns/ *n*. 天平，平衡

6 exploration /ˌeksplɔː'reiʃən/ *n*. 探险，考察，探测

7 threaten /'θretn/ *v*. 威胁；预示（某事）

8 organism /'ɔːgənizəm/ *n*. 生物体，有机体

9 create /kri'eit/ *vt*. 创造，创作；引起，产生

10 shrimp /ʃrimp/ *n*. 虾

Lesson

19

The stuff of dreams

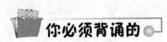 你必须背诵的

话说梦的本质

一项使人对这个问题感到困惑的奇怪的发现是，睡眠在很大程度似乎并不仅仅是为了使身体得到休息。

人体组织在一定程度上有自我修补和自我恢复的能力，有张有弛地连续活动时，其功能最佳。

平常人的睡眠周期中不时伴有一阵阵奇怪的眼球活动，这些活动有的飘忽而缓慢，有的急剧而快速。

这一切暗示我们：睡眠受到干扰没关系，而做梦受到干扰是有问题的。

 你一定熟读的

口语拓展一

People have been trying to discover what dreams mean for thousands of years. Ancient Greeks and Romans believed dreams provided messages from the gods. Sometimes people who could understand dreams would help military leaders in battle.

In ancient Egypt, people who could explain dreams were believed to be special. In the Christian Bible, there are more than seven hundred comments or stories about dreams. In China, people believed that dreams were a way to visit with family members who had died. Some Native American tribes and Mexican civilizations believed dreams were a different world we visit when we sleep.

In Europe, people believed that dreams were evil and could lead people to do bad things. Two hundred years ago, people awakened after four or five hours of sleep to think about their dreams or talk about them with other people. Then they returned to sleep for another four to five hours.

人们一直在试图发现梦的含义已经有几千年的历史了。古希腊人和罗马人认为，梦是从神那里向我们提供了消息。有时，能够理解梦的人也有助于在战场上的军事领导人。

在古埃及，人们把可以解释梦的人视为是非常特别的。在基督教的圣经里面，有超过 700 个评论或关于梦的故事。在中国，人们认为，梦是一种与过世家人相会的一种方式。一些美洲印第安人部落和墨西哥文明相信梦是当我们睡着的时候访问的一个不同的世界。

在欧洲，人们相信梦是邪恶的，可能导致人们做坏事。两百年前，人们醒后的四、五小时就会思考自己的梦，或者对与其他人谈论这些梦。然后又接着去睡另外四到五小时的觉。

口语拓展二

Knowledge is power, especially scientific and technological knowledge. Science and technology are the motive power of the social development. Without them human society could never have developed from primitive society to modern society. Therefore, to conquer and transform nature, we must master scientific knowledge.

However, social knowledge is also essential. Without it we can not understand society and don't know the law of the social development.

Therefore, besides scientific knowledge we need to master social science, philosophy, politics, history, aesthetics, etc, so that we can know society from all perspectives and form a correct world outlook.

知识就是力量，特别是科学和技术知识。科学技术是社会发展的原动力。没有它们，人类社会的发展永远无法从原始社会到现代社会。因此，要征服和改造自然，我们必须掌握科学知识。

然而，社会知识也很重要。没有它，我们无法理解社会，也不会知道社会发展的规律。因此，除了科学知识，我们还必须掌握社会科学、哲学、政治、历史、美学等，以使我们能够从各个角度了解社会，形成正确的世界观。

 你最好掌握的

1 comment /ˈkɔment/ *n*. 评论，意见，批评 *v*. 评论，谈论

2 civilization /ˌsivilaiˈzeiʃəns;-liˈz-/ *n*. 文明，文化

3 evil /ˈiːvl/ *a*. 邪恶的，坏的 *n*. 邪恶，罪恶

4 awaken /əˈweikən/ *v*. 唤醒，醒来，唤起

5 motive /ˈməutiv/ *n*. 动机，目的

6 primitive /ˈprimitiv/ *a*. 原始的，早期的；简单的，粗糙的

7 conquer /ˈkɔŋkə/ *v*. 克服，征服，战胜

9 transform /trænsˈfɔːm/ *v*. 转换，使……变形

10 essential /iˈsenʃəl/ *a*. 必要的，重要的，本质的

11 aesthetics /iːsˈθetiks/ *n*. 美学

12 perspective /pəˈspektiv/ *n*. 远景；看法；透视；前途，希望

72

Lesson

20 Snake poison

你必须背诵的

毒 蛇

　　蛇的唾液本来和我们人的消化液一样柔和，但经过漫长的时间，演变成了今天仍无法分析清楚的毒液。

　　毒液对毒蛇来说只不过是一种舒适生存的优越手段，它能够使蛇不用费多大的力气就能捕获到食物，轻咬一口即可。

　　不过，当它们相互撕打的时候，毒液就成了利弊参半的武器，可以杀死对方，也可以被对方的毒液杀死。

　　不同毒蛇的毒液产生的效果也不同，一种毒液作用于神经，另一种毒液作用于血液。

　　据说，神经毒液在两种毒液中是较原始的一种，而溶血性毒液，打个比方说是根据改良配方生产出的一种较新的产品。

你一定熟读的

口语拓展一

All snakes are carnivorous, eating small animals including lizards and other snakes, rodents and other small mammals, birds, eggs or insects. Some snakes have a venomous bite, which they do use to kill their prey before eating it. Other snakes kill their prey by constriction. Still others swallow their prey whole and alive. Most snakes are very easy to feed in captivity, apart from a minority of species.

Snakes do not chew their food and have a very flexible lower jaw, the two halves of which are not rigidly attached, and numerous other joints in their skull, allowing them to open their mouths wide enough to swallow their prey whole, even if it is larger in diameter than the snake itself. So it is a common misconception that snakes dislocate their lower jaw to consume large prey.

所有的蛇是肉食动物，它们吃一些小动物包括蜥蜴、其他种类的蛇、鼠和小的哺乳动物、鸟类、蛋或小昆虫。有些蛇是有毒的，它们利用这个技能在吃食物之前来杀死它们的猎物。没有毒液的蛇则通过紧压的手段来杀死猎物。当然还有一些是直接整个地吞掉猎物。大部分的蛇都很容易吃饱，除了一小部分的物种。

蛇不需要咀嚼它们的食物，因为它们有一个非常灵活的下颚，上下两部分都不是坚硬的连接在一起，它们的头骨有许多的关节，这就使它们能够张开它们的嘴巴来整个吞掉猎物，甚至是一些比蛇本身直径还要大的动物。所以说蛇是使它们的下颚变位来消耗食物，是一个很常见的误解。

口语拓展二

Snakes are long, thin reptiles. They do not have legs and they slither along the ground. Snakes have a long, legless, flexible body that is covered with dry scales. When snakes move about on land, they usually slide on their belly. Snake's eyes are covered by clear scales rather than movable eyelids; therefore, their eyes are always open. They repeatedly flick out their narrow, forked tongue, using it to bring odors to a special sense organ in the mouth.

Snakes belong to the order of animals called reptiles. This group also include crocodiles，lizards，and turtles. As with the other reptiles，snakes maintain a fairly steady body temperature by their behavior. They raise their temperature by lying in the sun or lower it by crawling into the shade.

Some snakes are ground dwellers，others live in trees，and other snakes spend most of their lives in water. There are a few areas where snakes do not live. They cannot survive in places where the ground stays frozen the year around，so they are missing in the polar regions or at high mountain elevations.

　　蛇是瘦而长的爬行动物。它们没有腿，沿着地面滑行。蛇有着长而且灵活的身躯，浑身布满了干干的鳞片。当蛇在陆地上活动的时候，通常是用腹部来进行滑行的。蛇的眼睛被一层很透明的鳞片所覆盖，而不是可以移动的眼睑。因此，蛇的眼睛总是睁开的。它们反复地伸出那个窄窄的，而且又分叉的舌头，通过它来把气味带到口中一个特殊的感官器官中。

　　蛇属于爬行类动物。爬行类动物还包括鳄鱼、蜥蜴和海龟。与其他爬行动物一样，蛇始终通过它的活动让自己身体保持相当稳定的温度。它们躺在阳光下提高自身的温度或爬到阴凉处降低它的温度。

　　有些蛇是陆地的住客，另一些生活在树上，还有一些蛇大部分时间生活在水中。还有一些地方蛇是不能生存的。它们无法生存在地面常年冻结的地方，所以蛇群在极地地区或在高海拔山区是很少的。

你最好掌握的

1 carnivorous /kɑːˈnivərəs/ *a.* 食肉的
2 mammal /ˈmæməl/ *n.* 哺乳动物
3 prey /prei/ *v.* 捕食，掠夺；折磨 *n.* 猎物，牺牲品

4 constriction /kən'strikʃən/ n. 压缩，收缩；限制，约束

5 captivity /kæp'tiviti/ n. 被俘；关押，监禁

6 minority /mai'nɔriti, mi-/ n. 少数，少数民族

7 flexible /'fleksəbl/ a. 灵活的，易弯曲的，柔韧的

8 jaw /dʒɔ:/ n. 颚，颌

9 rigidly /'ridʒidli/ ad. 严格地，坚硬地

10 halve /hɑ:v/ v. 分成两半，平分，减少到一半

11 misconception /'miskən'sepʃən/ n. 误解，错误想法

12 dislocate /'disləkeit/ v. 脱臼；使（交通，事物）混乱

13 consume /kən'sju:m/ v. 消耗，消费；大吃，大喝；烧毁

14 numerous /'nju:mərəs/ a. 为数众多的，许多

15 reptile /'reptail/ n. 爬行动物

16 slither /'sliðə/ v. 使……不稳地滑动（使……蜿蜒地滑行）

17 slide /slaid/ v. 使滑动，滑，跌落 n. 滑动，幻灯片

18 flick out 猛然伸出

19 odor /'əudə/ n. 气味，名声

20 organ /'ɔ:gən/ n. 风琴；机构；器官；新闻媒体

21 maintain /men'tein/ v. 维持，维修，保养，坚持

22 steady /'stedi/ a. 稳定的，稳固的；坚定的，不变的

23 dweller /'dwelə(r)/ n. 居民

24 elevation /ˌeli'veiʃən/ n. 提高，提升，提拔；海拔；（建筑物的）
立体图

25 survive /sə'vaiv/ v. 生存；比……的活得长

Lesson
21
William S. Hart and the early 'Western' film

 你必须背诵的

威廉·S·哈特和早期"西部"电影

总之，主人公是一个自相矛盾，又与他的拓荒环境相矛盾的人物。

他塑造的英雄人物深深地扎根于他本人的记忆和经历之中，也扎根于有关已经消失的拓荒生活的历史和神话之中。

哈特扮演的被误认为坏人的好人总是一个局外人，总是一个被剥夺继承权的人。

如今，不宣而战的侵略、战争、虚伪、诈骗、无政府状态以及即将临头的毁灭成了我们日常生活的一部分，我们都希望有一个赖以生存的行为准则。

 你一定熟读的

情景模拟对话一

A: Did you see the movie on channel 6 last night?
B: No. I missed it. I went shopping for clothes.
A: It was an excellent film. Especially we could watch it on television, you know.

B: I read the preview in yesterday's paper and hoped to watch it last night, but, then, Susan called me to go shopping with her. So I went.

A: You remember that the critic thought that it was one of the best films of the last ten years.

B: Yes. I do remember. He felt it would be a candidate for some awards at the end of the year.

A: Well, if I were one of the judges, I'd pick it as the best film of the year. I haven't seen such a marvelous plot and such superb acting for a long time!

B: Sounds as if I'll have to see it, if they ever re-run it.

A: 你昨晚看了六频道的电影吗?

B: 没有,我错过了,我去买衣服了。

A: 那部电影简直太棒了。你知道吧,尤其是在电视上能看到。

B: 我昨天在报纸上看了看预告,也是希望昨天晚上能看到,可是,苏珊叫我和她一起去逛街,所以我就去了。

A: 你记不记得那个影评家认为这是近十年来最好的电影之一。

B: 嗯,我记得。他认为这部电影在年底将成为一些奖项的候选。

A: 嗯,如果我是其中的一个评委,我会选它作为本年度最好的电影,我好久都没有看见这么完美的情节,这么优秀的表演了。

B: 听起来好像我不能不看它,如果他们能重播的话。

情景模拟对话二

A: What's the plot of your new movie?

B: It's a story about a policeman who is investigating a series of strange murders. I play the part of the detective. He has to catch the killer, but there's very little evidence. It's a psychological thriller with some frightening scenes, but I hope audience won't be too scared to go to the movie theatres!

A: Did you enjoy making the movie? We heard stories about disagreement with other actors and with the director.

B: I have had disagreement with every director. We've always disagreed in a friendly way and we have always resolved our differences. It was the same when I made this movie. I don't know where rumors of my disagreement with Rachel Kelly come from. We got on very well and I hope to work with her again. I enjoyed making the movie very much.

A: Critics are not very happy with the movies that you've made recently. Does that bother you?

B: Not at all. The feedback from audience has been great. I care about what they think more than what the critics think.

A: Did you do your own stunts in the movie?

B: I wanted to, but my insurance company wouldn't let me. All of my stunts were done by a stuntman. As you know, I used to do my own stunts, but I'll leave that to be an expert in future.

A: Thank you very much for doing this interview.

B: My pleasure. Have you seen the movie yet?

A: Yes. I have. I liked it very much. Like you, I was very impressed with Rachel's performance in the movie. She's going to be a star.

A: 你的新电影的故事情节是什么?

B: 是一部关于警察调查一些列的谋杀案的电影,我扮演那个侦探的角色,他必须抓住那个凶手,但是线索特别少。这是一个关于心理的惊险小说,里面有很多恐怖的画面,我只希望观众去电影院看的时候不要被吓到。

A: 你喜欢拍电影吗? 我听说一些关于演员与一些导演很不和的故事。

B: 我与每一个导演都是意见不一致。但是我们都是以友好的方式来争论,解决我们的分歧。这和我拍电影是一样的。我真不知道我与蕾切尔·凯利不和的谣言从哪来的。我们合作得非常愉快,而且还想和她再次合作。我非常喜欢拍电影。

A: 一些影评家们最近经常对你拍的电影评价不是很高。这些很影响你吗?

B: 一点也不。观众的反馈都很好的,比起他们的评论,我更在乎观众的想法。

A: 这部电影加上你自己专门的特技吗？

B: 我是想了，但是我的保险公司不允许。我所有的特技都是找的特技演员做的。你知道的，我以前经常做自己的特技。但是将来我可能不会做了，想以后成为一名这方面的专家。

A: 谢谢你为我们做的这次访谈。

B: 我的荣幸，你看没看这部电影？

A: 我看了，我非常喜欢。就像你说的一样，我对蕾切尔的表演留下了深刻的印象。她将来一定会成为大明星。

 你最好掌握的

1 excellent /'eksələnt/ *a.* 极好的，优秀的

2 preview /'pri:'vju:/ *n.* / *v.* 预展，试映，预演

3 critic /'kritik/ *n.* 批评家，评论家

4 candidate /'kændidit/ *n.* 候选人

5 award /ə'wɔ:d/ *n.* 奖，奖品 *v.* 授予，给予

6 judge /dʒʌdʒ/ *n.* 法官，裁判员，鉴定人 *v.* 审判；评判

7 marvelous /'maːviləs/ *a.* 令人惊异的，了不起的，不平常的

8 superb /sjuː'pəːb/ *a.* 极好的

9 plot /plɔt/ *n.* 阴谋，故事情节 *v.* 把……分成小块；绘制；密谋

10 investigate /in'vestigeit/ *v.* 调查，研究

11 evidence /'evidəns/ *n.* 根据，证据

12 scare /skɛə/ *n.* / *v.* 惊吓（惊恐，惊慌）

13 psychological /ˌsaikə'lɔdʒikəl/ *a.* 心理（学）的

14 thriller /'θrilə/ *n.* 惊险故事，戏剧，电影

15 disagreement /disə'griːmənt/ *n.* 不合，争论，不一致

16 resolve /ri'zɔlv/ *v.* 决定，解决，决心，表决

17 rumor /'ruːmə/ *n.* 谣言，传闻

18 feedback /'fiːdbæk/ *n*. 反馈

19 stunt /stʌnt/ *n*. 特技 *v*. 阻碍……的发育，成长；抑制，妨碍

20 insurance /in'ʃuərəns/ *n*. 保险

21 impress /im'pres/ *n*. 印象 *v*. 给……以深刻的印象；印，压

22 scene /siːn/ *n*. 场，景，情景

23 bother /'bɔðə/ *v*. 烦扰

Lesson

22

Knowledge and progress

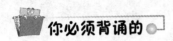 你必须背诵的

知识和进步

虽然人类在智力和道德上没有得到普遍提高，但在知识积累方面却取得了巨大的进步。

藏书使教育成为可能，而教育反过来又丰富了藏书，因为知识的增长遵循着一种"雪球法则"。

涓涓细流汇成了小溪，小溪现已变成了奔腾的江河。

所谓"现代文明"并不是人的天性平衡发展的结果，而是积累起来的知识应用到实际生活中的结果。

正像人们常常指出的，知识是一把双刃刀，可以用于造福，也可用来为害。

随着日益增长的知识的力量，如果我们继续利用知识的这种双重性，将会发生什么样的情况呢？

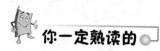

A: Hi! How are you doing?

B: I'm so stressed! I don't know where to go to school and what to major in!

A: Don't worry. You have plenty of time to decide.

B: If I want to get grants and scholarships to help me pay for tuition, then I need to apply on Monday.

A: Oh, I see. Well, let me see if I can help you. What's your favorite subject?

B: I like English, math, art, and music.

A: OK. Which one do you like the most?

B: I guess I'd have to say English. I usually do pretty well in English.

A: Which subject do you get your highest grades in?

B: Actually, that would have to be math.

A: OK, well. What kind of job do you want to get when you graduate?

B: I don't know. All I know is that I want to make lots of money!

A: Alright. So, is it more important to you to make money or to enjoy your work?

B: I would enjoy my world, not have to do much work, and make lots of money!

A: OK. Stop dreaming. Since you sound a bit unsure, I'd suggest that you should taking math and English classes in your first semester to see which you enjoy more. You can always change your mind.

B: That's a good idea. But what about deciding on where to go to college?

A: Why don't we go take a tour of some of the universities around here this weekend?

B: That sounds like a great idea, but to be honest, I've already decide that I don't want to go to school near home.

A: Oh? Why not?

B: I need to broaden my horizons. That's what you always say, right?

A: Yes, I support you.

A: 嗨，最近怎么样？

B: 压力挺大的。我都不知道去上哪个学校，要学什么专业？

A: 别担心，你还有很多时间决定呢。

B: 如果我想获得助学金和奖学金来帮助我支付学费，我就需要在星期一去申请了。

A: 噢，我明白了。嗯，让我看看我是否可以帮你。你最喜欢什么课程？

B: 我喜欢英语、数学、艺术和音乐。

A: 好的。哪一门课程最喜欢？

B: 我想我不得不说英语，我在英语方面表现得挺好。

A: 哪一门课程你得的分数最高？

B: 实际上是数学。

A: 好。你想你毕业时得到什么样的工作？

B: 我不知道。我只知道我想赚大钱！

A: 好吧，所以对你来说赚钱和享受生活更重要了，是吗？

B: 我要享受我自己的世界，没有太多的工作做，有好多的钱赚。

A: 好的。你别做梦了。因为听起来你有点不确定，我建议你在第一学期可以上数学和英语课程，看看你更喜欢哪个。你可以随时改变主意。

B: 好主意，但是怎么决定去哪个学校？

A: 为什么这周末我们不去周围一些大学参观考察呢？

B: 嗯，不错，不过说实话，我已经决定好了，我不想上家附近的大学。

A: 为什么？

B: 因为我想扩大我的视野，这也是你常说的，不是吗？

A: 是的，我支持你。

情景模拟对话二

A: I heard you were teaching English over there. Tell me about it.

Did you like it?

B: Oh，yes，it was very interesting.

A: What were the schools like?

B: Oh，I didn't actually teach in the schools. I taught in English institutes after schools.

A: But you taught children，yes?

B: Yes. That's right. But children in Taiwan are very different from children in America. At least as far as studying is concerned. Many children in Taiwan go to special institutes after school.

A: They actually study after school?

B: That's right. After their school day is over，they go to a special institute to study math or English. They are very serious about learning over there.

A: Hmm. That sounds pretty oppressive for the kids. Don't they ever relax?

B: Of course they do. Before I went over there I thought the same thing. I thought that maybe kids in Taiwan study too much. But now that I've worked there，and taught them，I feel it is a good thing. Their parents are very concerned about their education. More than American parents are. And that is good. American kids don't study enough.

A: Asian cultures value learning very much. I know that.

B: Are the kids in Taiwan very obedient?

A: That's a stereotype we Americans have. We think that Asian kids are very obedient and quiet. But it's not true. There are plenty of naughty kids too.

A: 听说你在那里教英文。说说看，你喜欢吗?

B: 是的，非常有意思。

A: 那是什么样的学校?

B: 我不是在学校教。我教课后的，在英语培训机构。

A: 你是教小朋友吧?

B: 是的，没错。不过台湾的小孩和美国的小孩非常不同。至少就读书来说是这样的。很多台湾的小孩在放学后都上补习班。

A: 他们放学后还学习?

B: 没错。放学后他们上补习班学数学或英文。在那里他们非常认真地学习。

A: 听起来相当压迫孩子，他们不休息吗?

B: 当然有休息。我去那里之前也是这么想。我认为台湾的小孩念太多书了。但是现在我在那里工作，教他们，我觉得这是好事。他们的父母非常关心孩子的教育，比起美国的父母要关心得多。那是好事，美国小孩念的书不是那么多。

A: 亚洲的文化非常看重学识，我知道这一点。

B: 台湾的小孩都很听话吗?

A: 那是我们美国人的刻板印象。我们认为亚洲小孩都很听话，很乖巧。不过这不是真的，也有很多顽皮的小孩。

你最好掌握的

1 stress /stres/ n. 紧张，压力；重力；重要性，强调 v. 重读，强调

2 scholarship /ˈskɔləʃip/ n. 奖学金，学识

3 tuition /tjuːˈiʃən/ n. 学费

4 horizon /həˈraizn/ n. 地平线

5 institute /ˈinstitjuːt/ n. 学会，学院，协会 v. 建立，制定；开始，着手

6 concern /kənˈsəːn/ n. 担忧，焦虑 v. 涉及，与……有关，影响；使关心

7 oppressive /əˈpresiv/ a. 压制性的，压迫的，沉重的

8 relax /riˈlæks/ v. 放松，松懈，松弛

9 obedient /əˈbiːdjənt,-diənt/ *a.* 服从的，顺从的

10 stereotype /ˈstiəriəutaip/ *n.* 铅版，陈腔滥调，老套 *v.* 把……模式化

11 naughty /ˈnɔːti/ *a.* 顽皮的，淘气的

Lesson

23 Bird flight

你必须背诵的

鸟的飞行方式

没有任何两种鸟的飞行方式是相同的。鸟的飞行方式千差万别，但大体上可分为两类。

信天翁是滑翔飞行的鸟类之王，它能自如地驾驭空气，但必须顺气流飞行。

这些肌肉以巨大的力量扇动短小的翅膀，使这类鸟能顶着大风飞行很远的路程才会疲劳。

这些鸟对我们是有益的，虽然我们不再从它们的飞翔姿态来占卜凶吉，连最迷信的村民也不再对喜鹊脱帽行礼，祝它早安了。

你一定熟读的

情景模拟对话一

A: Your dog is so much fun. It is so playful. I wish our cat enjoyed being around people as much as your dog does.

B: Cats are well known for being more independent than dogs. How old is your cat now? You've had its longer than we've had our

· 88 ·

dog.

A: It is eight years old and getting quite old. Your dog's six, isn't it?

B: Yes. It is so energetic. We take it out to the park every morning and evening. I think it would be happy to stay there all day!

A: I'm sure it would.

B: Your cat spends most of the day outdoors, right? Do you know where it goes?

A: It spends less time outdoors and it used to. We have no idea where it goes. It's very secretive. Occasionally, it brings back a dead mouse.

B: Have you ever thought about having another pet?

A: I never thought about it, I love my cat; I want take care of it all its life. It has become a member in my family.

A: 你的狗真是好有趣！我也希望我们家的猫也会喜欢在人多的周围，就像你们家的狗狗一样。

B: 猫比狗独立，这也是大家都知道的。你的猫几岁了？你养它的时间比我的狗长吧？

A: 它已经八岁了，已经很老了，你家的狗六岁，是吗？

B: 嗯，我的狗的精力还挺充沛呢。每天早上和晚上我都带它去公园。我想它很乐意整天呆在那里！

A: 我想它会的。

B: 你的猫经常在户外活动，你知道它去哪儿了吗？

A: 它本身在户外玩的时间就少，我们也不知道它去哪了，神神秘秘的，它还偶尔会带回来死的老鼠。

B: 你有没有想过再养其他的宠物？

A: 从来没有想过，我爱我的猫，我想照顾它一辈子，它已经成为我们家的一员了。

情景模拟对话二

A: I'm thinking about getting a pet, but I'm really not sure which animal would be suitable. Could you give me some advice?

B: Certainly! The first thing is to be honest about how much time you can devote to your pet. Dogs are very demanding. You need to take them for walks and they love to play. Cats, on the other hand, are more independent.

A: I'm fairly busy, so I really need an animal that I don't need to care of very much. Actually, I'd like a pet that's a little unusual. I don't really want a typical pet, like a cat, dog, or hamster. Do you have any suggestions?

B: Unusual pet are often more expensive to keep. Is that a problem?

A: Not really. By the way, I don't want a pet that could be dangerous, like a tarantula or rattlesnake.

B: We have those, but I only sell them to people I know well. How about a lizard? I have some that are very brightly colored, are not aggressive, and are easy to feed and look after.

A: That sounds ideal. Could you show me some?

B: Sure. Come over here. As you can see, I have a wide selection of species. They can live together, if you want lizards of different kinds. Do you have a favorite color?

A: I like the red one. What do they eat?

B: You can feed them on various things. They will eat small pieces of meat, but I'd recommend insects. You can get them from your garden, but remember that lizards eat a lot of insects.

A: Thanks a lot. What I'll do is find out more online and drop by next time.

B: That's fine. You shouldn't make a hasty decision when choosing a pet.

A: 我想养个小宠物，但是我真的不知道什么宠物合适，你能给我点意见吗？

B: 当然，首先你必须要明确自己有多少时间能够陪你的宠物。狗是很费心的，你必须领它们去散步，它们很喜欢玩。猫，相对而言显得更加独立。

A: 我很忙，所以我需要一个不会花费太多时间来照顾的小动物。

实际上，我喜欢特别一点的动物。我不太喜欢典型的动物，像是猫，狗或是仓鼠。你觉得呢？

B: 特别的动物通常要花费很多钱来养它，这个有问题吗？

A: 没问题，但是，话又说回来了，我不想养那种危险的动物像是蜘蛛或者响尾蛇之类的。

B: 我有一些，但是我都是卖给跟我很熟的人。蜥蜴怎么样？我这有一些颜色很亮的，而且没有攻击性也很容易喂养和照顾的。

A: 听起来很完美，你能带我去看看吗？

B: 当然，过来看看吧。就像你看到的，我有很多物种供你选择。如果你想要不同种类的品种，它们都可以在一起生活的。你喜欢什么颜色的？

A: 我喜欢红色的，它们都吃什么？

B: 你可以喂它们不同种类的东西，它们可以吃小片的肉。但是我还是推荐昆虫，你可以在花园中获取那些昆虫，但是记住蜥蜴需要吃大量的昆虫。

A: 十分感谢，现在我要做的就是上网再看看，然后下次再来拜访。

B: 没问题，选择饲养小动物不要做太草率的决定。

 你最好掌握的

1 independent /ˌindi'pendənt/ a. 独立的，自主的；不相关的，不相连的

2 energetic /ˌenə'dʒetik/ a. 精力旺盛的

3 secretive /si'kriːtiv/ a. 秘密的，偷偷摸摸的

4 occasionally /ə'keiʒənəli/ ad. 偶尔地

5 suitable /'sjuːtəbl/ a. 合适的，适宜的

6 devote /di'vəut/ v. 投入于，献身

7 demanding /di'mɑːndiŋ; (US) di'mændiŋ/ a. 要求多的，吃力的

8 typical /'tipikəl/ a. 典型的

9 hamster /'hæmstə(r)/ n. 仓鼠

10 tarantula /təˈræntjulə/ n. 一种大而有毒的蜘蛛

11 aggressive /əˈgresiv/ a. 侵犯的，攻击性的，挑衅的

12 recommend /rekəˈmend/ v. 建议，推荐，劝告，介绍

13 hasty /ˈheisti/ a. 匆匆的，轻率的，急忙的

Lesson

24　**Beauty**

你必须背诵的

美

日落处想必是通往遥远世界的大门。

虽然这光芒令人眼花缭乱，但它确实给予我们一种不曾经历和无法想象的美感和静谧的启示。

不可否认，一切伟大的艺术都具有使人遐想到进入天外世界的魅力。

一句话，如果美有某种意义的话，我们千万不要去阐明它的意义。

如果我们瞥见了只可意会不可言传的事物，企图把它说出来，那是不明智的。

对于我们不理解的事物，我们也不应该去赋予它某种意义。

你一定熟读的

情景模拟对话一

A: Could you tell me how much it is?

B: In the neighborhood of $ 500.

A: That's way too much money.

B: We can make down by model.

A: We have to ask for another price reduction.

B: You can forget about another cut.

A: How much are you asking for this?

B: I'm offering them to you at 10 Euro a piece. Is that all right?

A: Is tax already included in their price?

B: Yes. Our price can't be matched.

A: Would you consider a volume discount?

B: If you buy 1,000 or more, you'll get a 10% discount.

A: I'll accept your offer.

A: 您能告诉我这个的价格是多少吗？

B: 500 美元左右。

A: 价格太贵了。

B: 我们可以根据型号给予优惠。

A: 再给我们优惠点儿吧。

B: 不能再降价了。

A: 这个多少钱？

B: 每件 10 欧元，您看怎么样？

A: 这个价位含税吗？

B: 是的。我们的价格无人可比。

A: 批量购进可以再优惠吗？

B: 如果您能购进 1000 件以上我们就可以优惠 10%。

A: 好的，我接受。

情景模拟对话二

A: May I help you, Miss?

B: Yes. I'd like to look at lipstick and eye shadow.

A: What color set do you prefer?

B: Well, brown.

A: We have a beautiful selection of eye shadows this fall. Look at the colors. Aren't they beautiful?

B: But they're purple. I prefer a brown set.

A: If you insist, I can show you the brown sets. I'll have to warn you that they're very ordinary, though.

B: Well, I'm not so sure. Most of my make-up is brown.

A: Why don't you wear purple eye shadow for a change? We also have lipstick to go with it.

B: Can I try it?

A: Sure. Are you wearing any make-up?

B: No.

A: Have a seat, please. (She paints on eye shadow for her) Now, here is the mirror. How do you like it?

B: Not bad. Actually, it makes me look younger. I like it.

A: Try the lipstick as well.... See, how fresh and charming you look.

B: You're right. I'll take them all.

A: 小姐，我能为你做什么吗？

B: 嗯，我想看看口红还有眼影。

A: 你喜欢什么颜色呢？

B: 嗯，棕色吧。

A: 这个秋季，我们在眼影上有一个很不错的选择。看看这些颜色，漂亮吗？

B: 但是它们是紫色的，我喜欢棕色的。

A: 如果你坚持的话，我可以给你看棕色的，但是我不得不提醒你的是，棕色真的很普通。

B: 好吧，但是我大部分的化妆品都是棕色的。

A: 为什么不选择紫色来尝试着改变一下呢？我们同样有与它搭配的口红。

B: 我能试试吗？

A: 当然了。你化妆了吗？

B: 没有。

A: 请坐。（店员为她涂了眼影），好了，给你镜子，怎么样？喜欢吗?

B: 还不错，事实上，这个颜色让我看上去更年轻了，我很喜欢。

A: 也试试口红吧，看，你看上去多么清新迷人呀。

B: 没错，那我都要了。

 你最好掌握的

1　neighborhood /ˈneibəhud/ n. 附近，邻近

2　reduction /riˈdʌkʃən/ n. 减少，缩小

3　volume /ˈvɔljuːm；(US) -jəm/ n. 体积，容量，音量，卷，册

4　discount /ˈdiskaunt/ v. 打折扣 n. 折扣，数目

5　make-up /ˈmeikʌp/ n. 化妆品

6　insist /inˈsist/ v. 坚持，强调

7　selection /siˈlekʃən/ n. 选择，挑选

8　charming /ˈtʃɑːmiŋ/ a. 迷人的

Lesson
25
Non-auditory effects of noise

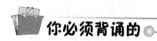
你必须背诵的

噪音的非听觉效应

要求减少噪音确实是件好事，但是如果与拙劣的科学掺杂在一起的话，就不会被人们所信任，这是很遗憾的。

即使住在离机场几英里以外的地方，机场的噪音也会使人难受。

对于噪音问题，需要对大量生活在噪音中的人进行研究，看一看他们是否比其他人更容易患精神病。

如果噪音对精神健康有影响的话，那也一定是微乎其微，以致现有的精神病诊断方法还发现不了。

你一定熟读的

情景模拟对话一

A: Hey, could you please turn down the radio?

B: No way. I've been waiting for this program for a long time.

A: But I want to take a nap.

B: Okay, I will put headphones on.

A: By the way, close the door, please.

B: Looks like you can't bear any noise when you sleep.

A: Of course not, can you?

B: Believe it or not, I can fall asleep while listening to rock music.

A: 嘿，能把收音机声调低点儿吗?

B: 没门。我等这个节目都等半天了。

A: 可我想睡会儿。

B: 好吧，我戴耳机吧。

A: 麻烦顺便把门关上。

B: 看来你睡觉时是听不得一点儿噪音啊。

A: 是睡不着，你能睡着?

B: 信不信由你，我听摇滚都能睡着。

情景模拟对话二

A: Is the environment a big issue in your country? It is in mine.

B: It is in mine too. The biggest issue is water. The climate is dry and so water conservation is very important.

A: What methods do you use to conserve water?

B: Water is rationed. We can only use a certain amount each month. It means that we cannot use some modern household items, like washing machines. They use too much water.

A: I see. I think the biggest environment problem in my country is air pollution.

B: Yes, I agree. The air here is much more polluted than in my country. Of course, my country is more agricultural and has much less industry.

A: We have reduced emission of air pollutants in recent years, but cars are still a major source of them. Factories have become cleaner as stricter environment pollution law have been introduced.

B: The problem is now on a truly global scale. I don't believe that any single country can do anything about it.

A: I think you're right. There needs to be an international response to this problem.

A: 环境在你们国家是一个大问题吗？在我们国家是。

B: 我们也一样，最大的问题就是水资源。气候很干燥，水资源保护是很重要的问题。

A: 保护水资源你们想采取什么方法？

B: 水是按定量供给的。我们每个月只用一定量的水。也就是说我们都不能用现代家居用品，像是洗衣机，那会很浪费水。

A: 我了解了，在我们国家最大的问题就是环境污染。

B: 嗯，我同意。这儿的空气比我们那里污染还要严重。当然，我们国家更多的是农业，而工业部分却很少。

A: 近几年，我们已经减少了对空气污染物的排放，但是汽车仍旧是最主要的来源。工厂已经变得更加干净，同时严格的环境污染法律也已经出台了。

B: 现在的问题真的都覆盖全世界了。我真的不相信任何一个单一的国家能够做什么。

A: 我想你说得很对，这是一个需要全世界回应的问题。

 你最好掌握的

1 nap /næp/ *n. / v.* 小睡，打盹

2 headphone /'hedfəun/ *n.* 戴在头上的耳机

3 conservation /ˌkɔnsə(ː)'veiʃən/ *n.* 保存，保护

4 conserve /kən'sə:v/ *n.* 蜜饯，果酱 *v.* 保存，保护，保藏

5 ration /'ræʃən/ *n.* 定额，定量，配给 *v.* 限量供应

6 pollute /pə'luːt,-'ljuːt/ *vt.* 污染

7 scale /skeil/ *n.* 鳞，刻度，数值范围，等级，天平 *v.* 刮去……的鳞片；称重；攀，爬

8 emission /i'miʃən/ *n.* 发射，发行；排放物

9 pollutant /pə'luːtənt/ *n.* 污染物质

Lesson

26

The past life of the earth

 你必须背诵的

地球上的昔日生命

只有生活在水中或者水边的动植物尸体最有可能被保存下来，因为保存的必要条件之一是迅速掩埋。

即使在有利的环境中，死去的生物中也只有一小部分能在开始腐烂前，或更可能在被食腐动物吃掉之前，被这样保存下来。

曾在陆地上生活过的动植物的遗体被保存下来的更为罕见，因为陆地上几乎没有什么东西覆盖它们。

 你一定熟读的

情景模拟对话

A: Do you think that climate changes is responsible for the recent floods?

B: It could be. There are floods in this country almost every year, but in recent years they have been more widespread and more frequent.

A: It seems that the climate in this country is changing.

B: The summers are hotter. The last three summers have been the hottest for the past 200 years. There have also been stronger winds.

A: I think that the changing climate is a sign that we are causing too much damage to the environment.

B: I think you're right. Climate changes naturally over time, but I think that human activities are speeding up the change. I wish that governments would join together and try to resolve the problem.

A: Me too. If we don't do something soon, it might be too late.

A: 你觉得气候变化是最近水灾的主要原因吗?

B: 可能是, 这个国家每年都有洪灾。但是最近几年好像分布更广, 而且发生频率更大了。

A: 看起来这个国家的气候正在变化。

B: 夏天很热。过去的三个夏天是 200 年以来最热的时期了。同样也会有很强的风。

A: 我想气候的改变是我们改变太多环境的信号。

B: 我觉得你说的没错。随着时间的推移, 气候环境在自然地改变, 但是我觉得人类的活动已经加快了这个改变, 我希望政府能够团结在一起, 努力解决这个问题。

A: 我也这么想。如果我们再不做点什么的话, 可能一切就会太迟了。

口语拓展

There are still many problems of environmental protection in recent years. One of the most serious problems is the serious pollution of air, water and soil. The polluted air does great harm to people's health. The polluted water causes diseases and death. What is more, vegetation had been greatly reduced with the rapid growth of modern cities.

To protect the environment, governments of many countries have done a lot. Legislative steps have been introduced to control air pollution, to protect the forest and sea resources and to stop any environmental pollution. Therefore, governments are playing the most important role in the environmental protection today.

To protect environment，the government must take even more concrete measures. First，it should let people fully realize the importance of environmental protection through education. Second，much more efforts should be made to put the population planning policy into practice，because more people means more pollution. Finally，those who destroy the environment intentionally should be severely punished. We should let them know that destroying environment means destroying mankind themselves.

目前环保还存在着许多问题。最严重的问题就是空气、水和土壤的严重污染。污染的空气对人类的健康十分有害。污染的水引起疾病，造成死亡。更有甚者，随着现代城市的迅速扩建，植被大大地减少。

为了保护环境，各国政府做了大量的工作。采用了立法措施控制大气污染，保护森林资源和海洋资源，制止任何环境污染。因此，政府在当今的环保中起着最重要的作用。

为了保护环境，政府应当采取更具体的措施。首先，应当通过教育的方法使人们充分意识到环境保护的重要性。第二，应更加努力把计划生育政策付诸实施，因为人口多就意味着污染严重。最后，要严惩那些故意破坏环境者。要使他们明白破坏环境就是毁灭人类自己。

你最好掌握的

1 responsible /ris'pɔnsəbl/ a. 有责任的，负责的
2 widespread /'waidspred,-'spred/ a. 分布（或散布）广的，普遍的
3 frequent /'fri:kwənt/ a. 经常的，频繁的
4 vegetation /ˌvedʒi'teiʃən/ n. 植物，草木
5 legislative /'ledʒisˌleitiv/ a. 立法的，有立法权的

6 concrete /ˈkɔnkriːt/ *a* . 具体的，实在的，有形的，明确的

7 realize /ˈriəlaiz/ *v* . 了解，实现

8 intentionally /inˈtenʃənli/ *ad* . 有意地，故意地

9 severely /siˈviəli/ *ad* . 严格地，激烈地

10 environmental /inˌvaiərənˈmentl/ *a* . 环境的

Lesson

27

The 'Vasa'

 你必须背诵的

"瓦萨"号

1628 年，一艘大帆船在处女航开始的时候就沉没了，这个从 17 世纪瑞典帝国流传至今的故事无疑是航海史上最离奇的事件之一。

人们从斯开波斯布朗和周围的岛屿前来观看这艘美丽的战船扬帆起航，乘风前进。

船头下浪花四溅，舰旗迎风招展，三角旗随风飘动，微风鼓起风帆，金碧辉煌的船楼闪耀着灿烂的色彩。

想要统治波罗的海的大型战舰"瓦萨"号，在它壮丽的起航时刻，带着全身飘扬的彩旗，沉没在了它诞生的港口。

 你一定熟读的

情景模拟对话一

A: What are you reading?

B: A holiday brochure.

A: Cool! Where're you going?

B: Greece. I just need my plane ticket and I'm off.

A: Don't you have to plan for visas, make hotel booking...?

B: No, my travel agent does that.

A: Hmm... My travel plans never seem to work out.

B: That's why I don't make plans. Then nothing can go wrong!

A: 你在看什么呢?

B: 度假手册。

A: 哇噢! 你要去哪里?

B: 希腊。我只要拿到机票就可以出发了。

A: 难道你不用办理签证,预定酒店……?

B: 不用,我的旅行代理会做的。

A: 嗯。我的旅行计划好像从来都不起作用。

B: 这就是为什么我不制定计划的原因,随遇而安吧!

情景模拟对话二

A: Hello, darling, are you all set? We have to go now.

B: Not yet. I'm still packing up things.

A: Darling, why are you taking such a big suitcase? It's only a 4 days' trip. Tell me what you put in here?

B: Our clothes, of course. I was told that it might be cold on the top of the mountain. So I take our light jackets with us.

A: Why are you taking towels and slippers? There are plenty in the hotel.

B: I prefer to use my own.

A: Why are you taking so many medicines?

B: Well, you never know what will happen. Remember you had a diarrhea last time we went to Jiu Zai Gou. Thanks god I brought imodium with me.

A: But darling why are you taking a mini fan with you?

B: It's very hot there. At least I can have some air wherever I go.

A: Anyway, we got to go or we will be late.

B: Wait a minute. I forgot the sunlight lotion. We definitely need it.

A: Darling, I am begging you. We got to go now. We always buy some things in the local areas, right?

B: Where is the camera? We can't go without a camera.

A: It's right on top of the drawer. Let me help you pack up.

B: OK. Where are our identification cards?

A: Oh, God, you remind me.

A: 亲爱的，你准备好了吗？我们得出发了。

B: 还没有呢，我还在收拾东西。

A: 亲爱的，为什么要拿那么大的箱子呢？我们只玩4天而已。里面都装了什么？

B: 当然是我们的衣服了，我听说晚上在山顶挺冷的，所以我带了薄夹克。

A: 为什么要带毛巾和拖鞋？宾馆里有好多的。

B: 我喜欢用自己的。

A: 为什么带那么多的药？

B: 你也不知道到那会发生什么，还记得上次我们在九寨沟你拉肚子吗？谢谢上帝让我带了盐酸洛哌丁胺的药。

A: 但是，亲爱的，你怎么把那个迷你风扇带着了？

B: 那儿很热啊，至少我们去哪儿都会有风陪伴吧。

A: 不管怎么样，我们必须得走了，否则就晚了。

B: 等一下，我忘记了防晒油，我们很需要它的。

A: 亲爱的，我求你了，我们得出发了，我们不是经常在当地也买一些东西吗？

B: 相机在哪？我们不能不带相机。

A: 在右边最上面的抽屉里。让我帮你收拾吧。

B: 我们的身份证你带了吗？

A: 天呐，你提醒我了。

 你最好掌握的

1 brochure /'brəuʃjuə/ *n*. 小册子

2 all set 准备就绪

3 pack up 打包，收拾

4 towel /ˈtauəl, taul/ n. 毛巾

5 diarrhea /ˌdaiəˈriə/ n. 痢疾，腹泻

6 slipper /ˈslipə/ n. 拖鞋

7 lotion /ˈləuʃən/ n. 洗涤剂；润肤霜

8 definitely /ˈdefinitli/ ad. 肯定地；明确地

9 identification /aiˌdentifiˈkeiʃən/ n. 身份的证明；认出；识别，辨认；鉴定

Lesson
28   **Patients and doctors**

 你必须背诵的

病人与医生

这是一个怀疑一切的时代，可是虽然我们对我们祖先笃信的许多事物已不太相信，我们对瓶装药品疗效的信心仍像祖辈一样坚信。

卫生部门的年度药费上升到了天文数字，并且目前尚无停止上升的迹象，这个事实证实了现代人对药物的信赖。

在医院门诊部看病的大多数人觉得，如果不能带回一些看得见，摸得着的药物，就不算得到充分的治疗。

并不只是那些无知没有受过良好教育的人才迷信药瓶子。

服药的最大优点是：除了暂时忍受一下令人作呕的味道外，对服药人别无其他要求。

 你一定熟读的

情景模拟对话一

A: Hello! How are you?

B: Not too well! I was just to see the doctor. I haven't been feeling too well over the last few days.

A: What have you got? A cough? A cold?

B: That's the funny thing. I don't what's wrong with me. I just feel exhausted.

A: Perhaps you've been working too hard. You do have a high-pressure job.

B: Maybe. I haven't been able to keep my food down either. That's unusual.

A: Well. I'm sure the doctor will be able to prescribe something to make you well again. Dr. Jameson is very good.

B: Yes, he is. I've make an appointment for 10 o'clock, so I'd better move along.

A: OK. Hope you feel better soon. You should take it easy.

A: 你好吗?

B: 不怎么好,我刚刚去看过医生,我已经有好几天都感觉不舒服了。

A: 你怎么了? 是咳嗽还是感冒?

B: 这也是很有意思的事情,我也不知道我怎么了,就是感到很疲倦。

A: 也许你工作太辛苦了吧,你工作的压力太大。

B: 也许吧,我把我吃的东西也都吐出来了,这看起来挺不正常的。

A: 嗯,我相信医生会给你开个药方,让你身体好转的,詹姆士医生很棒的。

B: 他的确很棒,我十点和他约好了,我想我该走了。

A: 好的,希望你很快好起来,你也别太紧张。

情景模拟对话二

A: Good morning. What seems to be the problem?

B: Good morning, doctor. I feel terrible. I've got a cold and I have a rash here on my neck. I'm not sleeping well either. What do you think the problem could be?

A: I'd say you've been working too hard or are under stress for some reason. Have you been taking anything for your cold?

B: Yes，I bought some medicine at the chemist's. I've been taking it for three days.

A: Good. I'm going to prescribe something stronger. It will make you feel drowsy，so you certainly should rest.

B: OK. I can afford to take a few days off work.

A: Have you been working hard recently?

B: Yes，I have. I had to get a project finished. It's done now, so I can relax a little.

A: Good. Let's take a look at that rash.... it looks worse. I'm going to prescribe some ointment for it. If the rash doesn't clear up in a few days，come back and see me. Do you have any other symptoms?

B: I have a bad headache，but...

A: Don't worry about that. It's probably of the stress you've been under. Just take some aspirin. Combined with the stronger cough medicine，it will make you feel very tired. You shouldn't work or use any equipment which requires concentration. If I were you, I'd just sleep, read a book, or watch TV. Here is your prescription.

B: Thanks doctor. I'll get these immediately. Goodbye.

A: 早上好，有什么问题?

B: 早上好，医生。我感觉不好，我感冒了而且脖子上有皮疹。我睡眠也不好，您说我这是有什么问题?

A: 你过去一段时间工作太辛苦了，或者是由于某种原因的压力。感冒中你有吃什么吗?

B: 嗯，我在药剂师那拿了些药，吃了有3天了。

A: 好，我会给你开些药性更强一点的，你可能会感觉总想睡觉，所以你必须休息。

B: 嗯，我能做到几天不上班。

A: 你最近工作很累吗?

B: 是的，我必须要完成一项工程，但是现在已经完成了，所以我可以休息一下。

A: 好，让我来看看这个红疹。它看上去还挺严重，我给你开点
药膏吧。如果几天之内还是没有消除的话，就回来找我你还
有其他的症状吗？

B: 我头有点疼，但是……

A: 不要担心，很可能是因为你压力太大了。吃一些阿司匹林吧。
然后再结合着吃点作用强的镇咳药，你可能会感到有些累。
你不要再工作了，也不要使用任何能让自己高度集中的设备。
如果我是你的话，我就睡睡觉，读读书或看看电视，这是你
的药方。

B: 谢谢您，医生，我马上去拿药，再见。

 你最好掌握的

1 appointment /əˈpɔintmənt/ n. 约会，预约；任命，委派

2 move along 走开，往前移动

3 rash /ræʃ/ a. 轻率的，匆忙的，鲁莽的 n. 疹子

4 chemist /ˈkemist/ n. 化学家，药剂师

5 drowsy /ˈdrauzi/ a. 昏昏欲睡的

6 ointment /ˈɔintmənt/ n. 药膏

7 symptom /ˈsimptəm/ n. 症状，征兆

8 concentration /ˌkɔnsenˈtreiʃən/ n. 集中，专心，专注

9 relax /riˈlæks/ v. 放松，松懈，松弛

Lesson

29

The hovercraft

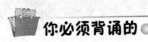
你必须背诵的

气 垫 船

本世纪已经研制出许多新奇的交通工具，其中最新奇的要数气垫船了。

他的设想是：用一个低压空气气垫或软垫来支撑船体，软垫周围用高压空气环绕。

他的解决办法是把船体提离水面，让船在一个气垫上行驶，气垫只有一两英尺厚。

后来气垫船跨越英吉利海峡，平稳地在波浪上方行驶，波浪不再产生阻力。

从那以后，各种各样的气垫船出现了，并开始了定期的航行服务。

未来的火车或许能成为"气垫火车"，靠气垫在单轨上行驶而不接触轨道，时速可达每小时 300 英里。

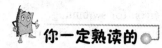 你一定熟读的

情景模拟对话一

A: I'd really like to go and see the swimming at the Olympics.

B: Yes, me too. I like the swimming, especially the... what's it called? You know when there are two swimmers together?

A: Synchronized swimming. I like that too.

B: I like it all — the races, the diving, and everything.

A: I want to try and get tickets for the swimming events.

B: Good idea. It would be great to see it live. The atmosphere will be fantastic.

A: 我非常想去看奥运会的游泳比赛。

B: 是的，我也是。我喜欢游泳，尤其是……那叫什么来着？你知道有两个游泳运动员在一起的项目？

A: 双人花样游泳。我也喜欢。

B: 我都喜欢——速度游泳、跳水，所有的一切。

A: 我想试试买游泳比赛的票。

B: 好主意。能够看到现场比赛的话太好了。气氛将非常热烈。

情景模拟对话二

A: Hurry up! Mom, I can't wait any more.

B: Look out, honey. Let's come to the shoal waters. Follow me!

A: OK, Mom. Can I swim now? I want to learn butterfly stroke.

B: Honey, listen to me. First, you should learn how to breathe in and breathe out.

A: Yes, I got you. It seems so easy. It's my turn to show off. Mom, it's so terrible. Water went down into my throat and I almost got drowned.

B: Do be patient, Honey. Let's do it slowly and correctly.

A: Oh，Mom，I think I'm not the right person for swimming.

B: Come on，sweetie，you've done very well. It is the first step that is tough.

A: Right，I'll make up my mind. Please correct me if any of my movements go wrong.

B: Yes，well done. That's the way to go. How clever you are! You've got it.

A: Really? I can't believe it. Everything is possible to a willing heart.

B: Exactly，next，you should hold your legs together and extend your arms above your head. OK，here we go. Then，kick your legs up and down together in a whipping motion generating from the hips and bending at the knees，as if you were a dolphin.

A: Yes，like a dolphin. Am I on the right track?

B: That's the way to go. Now，you are flying，my boy.

A: 快点妈妈，我等不及了。

B: 当心点，孩子。我们去浅水区吧，跟我来。

A: 好的，妈妈，我现在能游了吗? 我想学蝶泳。

B: 孩子，听我说，首先你得学会怎样吸气和呼气。

A: 嗯，知道了。好容易呀。轮到我大显身手了。妈妈，真糟糕。水到我的喉咙里来了，我差点被淹死。

B: 耐心点，孩子。让我们慢慢来，把它做好。

A: 好的，妈妈，我想我不是游泳的料。

B: 来吧，孩子。你做得很好了。万事开头难嘛。

A: 也是，我要加把劲。如果我动作做错了，就纠正我吧。

B: 对，做得好，就该这样。你多聪明呀! 你做对了。

A: 真的吗? 我简直不敢相信。有志者事竟成。

B: 对呀，下一步，把你的双脚合拢，把你的胳膊放到你的头上。好，这就对了。通过髋关节和膝关节用力运动，上下踢你的腿，就像海豚一样。

A: 嗯，像海豚一样。我做对了吗?

B: 对了。孩子，你进步了。

你最好掌握的

1 diving /'daiviŋ/ *n*. 潜水，跳水

2 shoal waters 浅水区

3 breathe /briːð/ *v*. 呼吸

4 patient /'peiʃənt/ *a*. 有耐心的，能忍耐的

5 extend /iks'tend/ *v*. 扩充，延伸，伸展，扩展

6 whipping /'(h)wipiŋ/ *n*. 鞭打（作为惩罚）

7 motion /'məuʃən/ *n*. 打手势，示意，动作 *v*. 运动，向……打手势

8 generate /'dʒenəˌreit/ *v*. 产生，发生

9 bend /bend/ *v*. 弯曲，屈服

Lesson

30

Exploring the sea-floor

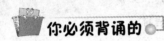 **你必须背诵的**

海底勘探

100 年前，我们只知道海洋是二维平面形的，以及靠近陆地浅水区的深浅不一能给航行带来危险。

无边无际的海洋深邃而神秘，凡是稍稍想过大海海底的人大概都会认为海底是平坦的。

大陆是崎岖不平的高地，高出辽阔海洋海底近三英里。

从海岸线向大海延伸几英里到几百英里的区域是大陆架慢坡，从地质学上来说，它是大陆的一部分。

大陆和海洋的真正分界线是在陡坡脚下。

 你一定熟读的

情景模拟对话一

A: How many styles of swimming do you know?

B: I know there are freestyle, back-stroke, breaststroke and butterfly.

A: What's the advantage of freestyle?

B: Swimming freestyle can build your shoulder muscles.

A: It sounds great. Do you know the order of medley relays?

B: Yes. In medley relays, each swimmer swims one stroke for the set distance; the order is back-stroke, breaststroke, butterfly and freestyle.

A: 你知道几种游泳姿势?

B: 我知道有自由泳、仰泳、蛙泳和蝶泳。

A: 自由泳有什么好处?

B: 自由泳可以锻炼你肩部的肌肉。

A: 听起来不错，你知道混合泳接力赛的顺序吗?

B: 是的，在混合泳接力赛中，每位运动员以一种姿势游一定距离，顺序依次是仰泳、蛙泳、蝶泳和自由泳。

情景模拟对话二

A: Hey, Daniel, how's it going?

B: Hey, Daddy, today I had really a fantastic history class.

A: Wow, it's so strange for you to say things like that. What had happened?

B: We've learnt the story of Zheng He "Sailing to West Ocean". He is a real great navigator.

A: Did your teacher tell you the route he took?

B: Yeah, he, with his fleet, came across the Indian Ocean, and arrived at the east coast of Africa.

A: Great, do you still remember when he started his voyage?

B: Of course, he started his voyage from 1405 to 1433, which is in Ming dynasty.

A: Good, by the way, do you finish reading the book *Robinson Crusoe* I've bought for you?

B: Not yet, you know I have a lot of homework to do.

A: You should speed up, because the story of Robinson can give you a better understanding about what you learned today.

B: OK, great Daddy, after supper, I'll embark on it.

A: That's my boy! Wait, Daniel, when is Pirates of the Caribbean on?

B: Is it about Captain Jack Sparrow, who wants to find the treasure on the sea?

A: Exactly, now, tell me the time.

B: I won't tell you, unless you promise to let me watch it with you.

A: 嗨，丹尼尔，怎么样了？

B: 嗨，爸爸。今天我上了一堂超棒的课。

A: 哇，你能说这种话太奇怪了。发生什么事情了？

B: 我们学了郑和下西洋的故事。他真是个伟大的航海家。

A: 老师告诉你他的航海路线了吗？

B: 是的，他跟他的舰队穿过了印度洋到达了非洲东海岸。

A: 好的，你记得他什么时候开始的航行的？

B: 当然，从1405~1433年，那是在明朝时期。

A: 好的，问一下，你读完了我给你买的那本《鲁滨逊漂流记》了吗？

B: 还没有，你知道我有很多家庭作业要做。

A: 你应该加快速度，因为鲁滨逊的故事能够帮助你理解今天所学的东西。

B: 好的，伟大的父亲大人，晚饭后，我就开始。

A: 这才是我的孩子，等等，丹尼尔，《加勒比海盗》什么时候开演？

B: 是不是关于想在海上找到宝藏的杰克船长？

A: 对啊，告诉我时间。

B: 除非你答应我跟你一起看，我才告诉你。

 你最好掌握的

1 medley relay 混合泳

2 freestyle /ˈfriːstail/ n. 自由式

3 fantastic /fæn'tæstik/ *a.* 极好的，难以相信的，奇异的

4 navigator /'nævigeitə/ *n.* 航海家

5 fleet /fli:t/ *n.* 船队，舰队

6 embark /im'bɑ:k/ *v.* 乘船，着手，从事

7 route /ru:t/ *n.* 航线，路线

Lesson

31

The sculptor speaks

雕塑家的语言

对雕塑的鉴赏力取决于对立体的反应能力。雕塑被说成是所有艺术中最难的艺术,可能就是这个道理。

正在学看东西的儿童起初只会分辨二维形态,不会判断距离和深度。

虽然他们对平面形式的感觉能达到相当准确的程度,但他们没有在智力和情感上进一步努力去理解存在于空间的整个形态。

他的大脑能从物体的各个角度勾画出其复杂的形象,他看物体的一边时,便知道另一边是个什么样子。

他能意识到物体的体积,那就是它的形状在空气中所占的空间。

敏锐的雕塑观赏者也必须学会把形体作为形体来感觉,不要靠描述和联想去感觉。

 你一定熟读的

情景模拟对话一

A: I like this copy very much. How much does it cost?

B: It's the most expensive one in the shop. It costs five hundred Yuan.

A: That's too expensive for us.

B: This one is less expensive than that one. It's only three hundred Yuan. But, of course, it's not as good as the expensive one.

A: I don't like this one.

B: The other one is more expensive, but it's worth the money.

A: 我非常喜欢这件复制品。请问它多少钱?

B: 这是店里最贵的一种。它的售价是 500 元。

A: 这对我们来说是太贵了。

B: 这件比那件要便宜些。它只要 300 元。但是,它当然没有价钱高的那种好。

A: 我不喜欢这种。

B: 那一种价格是贵一些,但它值这么多钱。

情景模拟对话二

A: Wow, your city has changed a lot, I couldn't simply recognize it.

B: When did you come to Shanghai last time?

A: Ten ages ago.

B: No wonder you say so. During the past ages our government has be preparing for the Expo 2010.

A: "Better City, Better Life" is the theme of the Expo?

B: Right. It's a dream. All the Shanghai human are working exert to do the dream coming true.

A: I believe the Expo is bound to achieve a complete success.

B: Thank you.

(Suddenly the taxi slows down.)

A: What's the matter? Have we arrived?

C: No, no. As it's the rush hour, we at whiles get trapped in traffic jams.

A: Will we be here for long?

C: Don't worry. It won't get more than 5 minutes, I consider.

A: Really? Outside is like a huge crowd of human.

B: Actually, our traffic condition has been outstandingly improved. It can meet the demand of transporting not less than 150,000 human per peak hour. So, get it easy, please.

C: What's abundance, as our government was planned, the Expo is located at the outer areas of the central city district. Therefore, the traffic is very convenient.

A: Your government did a good job.

B: Quite right. Ha, we have arrived.

A: Oh, how magnificent! How much do I owe you?

C: Seventy-five Yuan.

A: OK, here's eighty Yuan. Keep the change.

C: Thanks a lot. Enjoy the exhibition!

A: 哇, 你们的城市变化真大, 我简直都认不出来了。

B: 你上次是什么时候来上海的?

A: 10 年前。

B: 难怪你会这么说。这些年来我们政府为了 2010 年世界博览会的召开做了大量的准备工作。

A: (望着一块广告牌) "城市, 让生活更美好", 这是这次世界博览会的主题吗?

B: 是的。这是一个梦想。所有的上海人都在为梦想成真而努力工作着。

A: 我相信这次世界博览会一定会取得圆满成功的。

B: 谢谢。

(突然间。出租车慢了下来。)

A: 怎么回事? 我们到了吗?

C: 不, 不是。因为现在是高峰时段, 所以有时交通比较阻塞。

A: 我们会被困在这儿很久吗?

C: 别担心。不会超过 5 分钟的, 我想。

A: 真的吗? 外面的人可真多啊。

B: 事实上，我们的交通状况已经大大改善了。如今可以保证高峰时段不少于 15 万的人流通畅行无阻。所以，不用紧张。

C: 而且，正如我们政府当初所规划的，世界博览会会区位于上海市中心地区的外环，因此交通十分便利。

A: 你们政府干得真不错。

B: 是啊。哈，我们到了。

A: 哦，真宏伟啊！我要付你多少钱？

C: 75 元。

A: 好的，这里是 80 元。不用找了。

C: 谢谢，祝你们观展愉快！

 你最好掌握的

1 worth /wəːθ/ *n*. 价值，值……钱，值得……的

2 recognize /ˈrekəgnaiz/ *v*. 认出，认可，承认

3 theme /θiːm/ *n*. 题目，主题

4 exert /igˈzəːt/ *v*. 发挥，运用；用力，尽力

5 bound /baund/ *n*. 跳跃，界限，范围 *v*. 跳跃；弹回；限制 *a*. 受约束的，装订的，有义务的

6 trap /træp/ *v*. 设圈套，设陷阱；困住；使受限制 *n*. 圈套，陷阱

7 outstandingly /ˈautˈstændiŋli/ *ad*. 醒目地

8 locate /ləuˈkeit/ *v*. 找出，设于，位于

9 magnificent /mægˈnifisnt/ *a*. 壮丽的，宏伟的

Lesson

32

Galileo reborn

 你必须背诵的

伽利略的复生

但是相比之下，对于科学史学家来说，伽利略只是在现代才变成一个新的难题。

他首先是个实验工作者，他蔑视亚里士多德学派的偏见和空洞的书本知识。

他是第一个把望远镜对准天空的人，观察到的论据足以把亚里士多德和托勒密一起推翻。

今天，虽然已故的伽利略继续活在许多通俗的读物中，但在科学史家中间，一个新的更加复杂的伽利略的形象出现了。

伽利略用望远镜所作的观察确实是不朽的，这些观察在当时引起了人们极大的兴趣，具有重要的理论意义。

 你一定熟读的

情景模拟对话

A: Do you believe that there're aliens lived in distant outer space?

B: Not only believe, but I'm also fascinated with the idea.

A: Oh! Really? That's awesome. I believe in it too.

B: There're so many planets in the universe. As a human, we cannot be alone.

A: That's right. I believe there'll be plenty of aliens come to earth in the future. No matter what they come for, I'd like to meet them.

B: I think they must be ugly.

A: Maybe you're right. Or perhaps we don't share the same aesthetics.

B: Whatever, I want to make friends with them. How about you?

A: That makes the two of us.

A: 你相信在遥远的外太空有外星人吗?

B: 我不仅仅相信，而且我对这个想法还很痴迷。

A: 噢! 真的吗? 那太好了，我也相信有外星人在宇宙中!

B: 宇宙中有那么多星球。作为地球人，我们不可能是孤独的!

A: 没错。我相信在未来有很多外星人会来地球。不管是什么目的，我都很想见见他们!

B: 我想他们一定长得很丑陋!

A: 可能是吧。也许我们的审美观不同!

B: 总之，我想和他们做朋友。你呢?

A: 一样!

口语拓展

Man has been fascinated by outer space for thousands of years. It has been almost over forty years since man's first landing on the moon. Now, some people believe that space exploration is a sheer waste of time and money, they point out the face that it cost billions of dollars to carry on the space research, but a little information was brought back. Many new products, such as weather and communication satellites, are also products of space programs, and they have benefited people all over the world. And what's more, scientific knowledge about outer space has been acquired by mankind.

We believed that it will bring more benefits in the future, which we can not even imagine now. Space exploration is a challenge to human beings. That's why several nations try hard to carry out space exploration continuousl.

人类对外部空间着迷已有上千年的历史了。从人类第一次登上月球起至今已有四十多年了。现在，有些人认为空间探索完全是浪费时间和金钱。他们指出，数百亿美元用于太空研究，但收获甚微。许多新产品，如气象、通信卫星都直接得益于空间研究，使全球受益匪浅。而且人类从中获得了不少关于太空的知识，我们相信，将来它会带给人类更多的好处，有些甚至是我们现在无法想象的。太空探索对我们人类来说是个挑战，这也是为什么许多国家不断进行探索的原因之一。

 你最好掌握的

1 fascinate /ˈfæsineit/ v. 使……着迷，使极感兴趣
2 exploration /ˌeksplɔːˈreiʃən/ n. 探险，考察，探索
3 continuously /kənˈtinjuəsli/ ad. 不断地，连续地

Lesson

33

Education

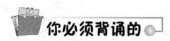

教　育

　　我们许多人都相信，一个没有受过教育的人，是逆境的牺牲品，被剥夺了 20 世纪最优越的机会之一。

　　如果我们的教育制度仿效没有书籍的古代教育，我们的学院将具有可以想象得出的最民主的形式了。

　　在原始文化中，寻求和接受传统教育的义务对全民都有约束力，因而没有"文盲"。

　　那里没有我们今天社会中的匆忙生活，而匆忙的生活常常妨碍个性的全面发展。

　　人们没有必要离家谋生，所以不会产生孩子无人管的问题，也不存在父亲无力为孩子支付教育费用而犯难的问题。

你一定熟读的

情景模拟对话一

A: Excuse me, do you know where the visa office is?

B: Yes, I do. I'll walk you there.

A: Thanks!

B: Are you applying to study or work abroad?

A: I want to study abroad.

B: What do you want to study?

A: I hope to study English literature.

B: Have you got your visa yet?

A: Not yet. I have an interview with the visa official today.

B: I see. Is it your first interview?

A: Yeah. Like most students. I want to work in America after graduation.

B: I see. Well, good luck!

A: 打扰了，你知道办签证的办公室在哪里吗？

B: 我知道，我带你过去。

A: 谢谢。

B: 你要申请出国学习还是工作？

A: 出国留学。

B: 你想学什么呢？

A: 我想学英国文学。

B: 你曾经得到过签证吗？

A: 还没有，今天我就是来这面试的。

B: 我知道了，这是你第一次面试？

A: 是的。像所有的学生一样，我想毕业后在美国工作。

B: 我知道了，好了，祝你好运！

情景模拟对话二

A: Guess what came in the mail today?

B: What?

A: My acceptance letter to Yale!

B: Wow! Congratulation! When do classes start?

A: Freshman orientation is the last week of August, but I want to go two weeks before that to get settled in.

B: You're so lucky! Do you have to do many things before you leave?

A: Yes. I'll be very busy! I have to get a visa, buy a plane ticket, and pack my things. But first, I want to register for class.

B: When can you do that?

A: Well, they sent me their prospectus, so I can start looking now. Do you want to help me decide which classes to take?

B: Sure. What can you choose from?

A: Well, I have to take all the fundamental courses, plus a few from my major.

B: What is your major?

A: I hope to major in English literature, but the admission's counselor told me that many people change their major times in their first year.

B: What are the fundamental courses?

A: In order to graduate, every student must take a certain amount of classes in history, math, English, philosophy, science and art.

B: Interesting. That's very different from the Chinese education system.

A: Yes, it is. It's also very different from the British education system.

B: Really?

A: Oh, sure. In British, students don't have to take the foundation course.

B: Why not?

A: Maybe because they think they know everything already! HaHa.

A: 猜猜我今天收到了什么邮件?

B: 什么?

A: 耶鲁大学的通知书。

B: 哇，恭喜你，什么时候上课?

A: 新生训练营在 8 月的最后一个星期开始，但是我想提前两个星期去，提早安顿下来。

B: 你好幸运呀! 走之前还有很多事情要做吧?

A: 是呀，我想我会非常的忙，我要办签证，买飞机票，收拾东西，但是现在最主要的是登记班级。

B: 什么时候开始做?

A: 嗯, 他们给我发了简章, 我正在看, 你想帮我来看看我要选什么课吗?

B: 当然, 从哪开始选呢?

A: 嗯, 我必须要选择所有的基础课, 还有一些我的专业?

B: 你想主修什么?

A: 我希望我能主修英语文学。但是那个录取办的顾问告诉我他们第一年的时候会经常换专业。

B: 基础课程都有什么呢?

A: 为了毕业, 每个学生都必须在历史、数学、英语、哲学、科学和艺术上学习一定的课程。

B: 很有意思, 这也是和中国的教育系统很不相同的地方。

A: 是啊, 和英国的教育系统也不一样。

B: 真的吗?

A: 当然了, 在英国, 学生都不用非得学习基础课。

B: 为什么不学?

A: 可能他们都认为什么都知道了吧。哈哈。

你最好掌握的

1 visa /ˈviːzə/ v. / n. 签证

2 acceptance /əkˈseptəns/ n. 接受, 容纳; 赞成

3 orientation /ˌɔː(ː)rienˈteiʃən/ n. 方向, 目标, 适应

4 register /ˈredʒistə/ v. 记录, 登记, 注册 n. 登记表

5 prospectus /prəsˈpektəs/ n. 章程, 简章, 样张

6 fundamental /ˌfʌndəˈmentl/ a. 基本的, 根本的 n. 基本原理

7 literature /ˈlitəritʃə/ n. 文学, 文献

8 admission /ədˈmiʃən/ n. 许可, 入场券, 承认

9 counselor /ˈkaunsələ/ n. 顾问, 参事, 法律顾问

10 amount /əˈmaunt/ n. 数量, 总额 v. 总计, 等于

11 plus /plʌs/ n. 加号, 正号 prep. 加上, 另有 a. 正的

Lesson

34

Adolescence

 你必须背诵的

青 春 期

当家长听到孩子赞扬自己朋友家时，总感到不安，认为这是孩子在嫌弃自家的饭菜、卫生或家具，而且愚蠢地让孩子看出自己的烦恼。

不管家长的人品有多好，作为父母又多么合格，孩子们对家长幻想的破灭在某种程度上是不可避免的。

孩子们所不能原谅的是：父母错了，孩子们也看出来了，可是做父母的还不肯承认。

他们可以靠无理的独断专行来维护自己的尊严，实际上那是根本不行的。

遇事采取面对现实的态度总是比较明智和稳妥的，尽管会有暂时的痛苦。

 你一定熟读的

情景模拟对话一

A: Tommy played truant today. His teacher called me this morning.

B: Where did he go?

A: I've asked him, but he won't tell me. What should we do about this? He is like you. I remember we were at the college you always skip classes.

B: Like me? But you see, I'm so successful now, and if he is really like me, he'll be more successful than me in the future.

A: Stop, stop. We're talking about our son's attendance for classes and his study. Maybe we can give him a little bit of money to pay him to go to school.

B: Pay him? But he studies for himself, not for you or for me or for anybody else. I've got an idea. You should send him to class every morning, and then you go to work.

A: In that way, I'll be late every day. How about letting him go to school on school bus?

B: That's a good idea! Why have I never thought of that?

A: That's because I went to school for each class when I was at school, so now I am much more clever than you.

A: 汤米今天逃学了。他的老师今天早上给我打电话了。

B: 他去哪里了?

A: 我问过他,但是他没告诉我。我们该怎么做呢?他就和你一样,我记得我们上大学的时候你就总是逃课。

B: 像我?但是你现在看看,我现在都已经成功了。如果他像我的话,那么他将来一定会比我更成功。

A: 别说了,我们正在讨论的是儿子的逃课,还有他的学习。也许我们可以给他点钱,让他去上学。

B: 给他钱?学习是他自己的事情,不是为我,为你,为任何人学习的。我有个好主意,我想你每天早上送他去上学,然后再去上班。

A: 这样的话,我上班会迟到的,为什么不让他坐校车呢?

B: 好主意,为什么我没有想到呢?

A: 那是因为我上学的时候每节课都会去,所以现在我比你聪明。

情景模拟对话二

A: In your mind, what do you think of the generation gap always appearing between parents and children?

B: First, parents and children often fail to talk with each other. At most time, they do not think the others' ideas deeply; instead, they would let them alone. By doing this, they send false messages to each other. As the result, the two different worlds meet head on and the generation gap appears.

A: Oh, I see. How to solve the generation? What should we do about it?

B: For the parents, I think they should treat their children as friends. After all, they are young and they have their own ideas. Whether they are wrong or not, parents should expect their children's ideas. If they are truly wrong, parents should have patience and make children to realize their mistakes earnest.

A: That's right. I agree with you.

B: Of course, children also accept their parents' suggestions and try to hard to get rid of their disadvantages. From another aspect, if parents treat their children rudely, they may get into trouble. The reason is very simple, children hate the bad measures parents take. In this way, the distances between them will become further and further.

A: I think I understand you. You want to say that parents should have patience and respect to their children, right?

B: That's really what I want to express. You know, if the children didn't make mistakes, parents shouldn't ask them more questions again and again. Just let them know what they want to do and hope their parents accept them possible.

A: I know it. And the most important one thing is we all hope parents should give us more room of ourselves. We need freedom. But I'm afraid that's not an easy thing to solve.

B: Of course, the generation gap is really difficult to settle.

A: 根据你的想法，你认为经常发生在孩子和父母之间的代沟的原因是什么？

B: 首先，父母和孩子经常谈话以失败告终。很多时候，他们不能深刻地理解彼此的想法。相反，他们却置之不理。通过这么做，就给了彼此错误的信息。这样，两种不同的世界就碰撞在一起，代沟也随之产生了。

A: 嗯，我知道，那如何解决代沟的问题呢？我们该怎么做呢？

B: 对父母而言，我想他们应该对待孩子像对待朋友一样。毕竟，他们年轻而且有自己的想法。不管他们的想法是对还是错，父母都应该尊重孩子的想法。如果孩子真的错了，父母应该很耐心、很认真地让孩子认识到错误。

A: 没错，我同意。

B: 当然，孩子也要接受父母的建议，努力改正自己的不足。从另一方面讲，如果父母对孩子太粗鲁的话，他们就会有麻烦了。原因很简单，孩子讨厌父母这样的方式。如果这样的话，父母和孩子之间的距离也会越来越远。

A: 我理解，你的意思是说，父母应该耐心，并且要尊重孩子，是吗？

B: 这是我真正想表达的。你知道的，如果孩子没有犯错，家长就不应该一遍遍的问孩子问题。应该让父母知道他们想要做什么，而且要尽可能地接纳他们。

A: 我知道，而且最重要的是我们都希望父母能够给我们足够的空间。我们需要自由，但恐怕这不是一件容易解决的事情。

B: 当然了，代沟问题本来就很难解决。

你最好掌握的

1 truant /ˈtruːənt/ n. 懒惰鬼，旷课者

2 skip /skip/ v. 跳越，跳过；略过；跳蹦 n. 跳，蹦跳

3 attendance /əˈtendəns/ *n.* 出席

4 generation gap 代沟

5 solve /sɔlv/ *v.* 解答（难题），解决

6 patience /ˈpeiʃəns/ *n.* 耐心

7 settle /ˈsetl/ *v.* 安放，安顿，定居，解决

Lesson

35

Space odyssey

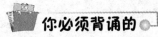 你必须背诵的

太空探索

从月球上的岩石中很容易提炼出液态氧，作为航天飞船的燃料。

要乘坐一枚火箭飞离地球，火箭的速度要达到每秒 7 英里，而从月球出发的相应速度只是每秒 1.5 英里。

火星对未来的星际旅客来说有着特殊的魅力。

这是一个红色沙漠的世界，无云的天空，凶猛的沙暴，比大峡谷还宽的裂缝，起码有一座山有珠穆朗玛峰的近两倍高。

 你一定熟读的

口语拓展一

The ideas which had grown over two thousand years of observation have had to be radically revised. In less than a hundred years, we have found a new way to think of ourselves. From sitting at the center of the universe, we now find ourselves orbiting an average-sized sun, which is just one of millions of stars in our own Milky Way galaxy. And our galaxy itself is just one of billions of galaxies, in a universe that is infinite and expanding. But this is far from the end of a long history of inquiry. Huge questions remain to be answered, before we can hope to have a complete picture of the universe we live in. Our image of the universe today is full of strange sounding ideas, and remarkable truths. The story of how we arrived at this picture is the story of learning to understand what we see.

过去2000多年的观察所孕育出来的观点不得不更改一新。在不到100年的时间里，我们找到了审视我们自己的新方法。过去我们自认为是宇宙的中心，现在发觉我们围绕一颗体积中等的太阳在转，而太阳只是银河系中数百万颗恒星中的一颗。而我们的星系又只是数百万个星系中的一个，存在于无穷无尽、不断扩展的宇宙中。但这远没有解决我们长久以来的疑问。很多重大问题尚未得到解决，更别说要完全了解我们生活的宇宙的全貌。我们今天的宇宙观充满前所未知的观点和引人注目的真知灼见。我们形成这样的宇宙观的过程也就是我们学会理解耳闻目睹的一切的过程。

口语拓展二

Man has been fascinated by outer space for thousands of years. It has been almost over forty years since man's first landing on the moon. Now, some people believe that space exploration is a sheer waste of time and money. They point out the fact that it cost billions of dollars to carry on the space research, but a little information was brought back.

However, every coin has two sides. There are still a majority of other people who believe that space exploration has more advantages. Many new products, such as weather and communication satellites, are also products of space programs, and they have benefited people all over the world. And what's more, scientific knowledge about outer space has been acquired by mankind.

We believed that it will bring more benefits in the future, which we can not even imagine now. Space exploration is a challenge to human beings. That's why several nations try hard to carry out space exploration continuously.

人类对外部空间着迷已有上千年的历史了。从人类第一次登上月球起至今已有 40 多年了。现在，有些人认为空间探索完全是浪费时间和金钱。他们指出，数百亿美元用于太空研究，但收获甚微。

然而，任何事物都具有两面性。仍有大多数人认为进行空间探索利大于弊。许多新产品，如气象、通信卫星都直接得益于空间研究，使全球受益匪浅，而且人类从中获得了不少关于太空的知识。

我们相信，将来它会带给人类更多的好处，有些甚至是我们现在无法想象的。太空探索对我们人类来说是个挑战，这也是为什么许多国家不断进行探索的原因之一。

 你最好掌握的

1 observation /ˌəbzəːˈveiʃən/ *n*. 观察

2 radically /ˈrædikəli/ *ad*. 根本地，完全地

3 revise /riˈvaiz/ *v*. 校订，修正；复习

4 galaxy /ˈgæləksi/ *n*. 银河系；星系；杰出的人物

5 remarkable /riˈmɑːkəbl/ *a*. 显著的，异常的，非凡的，值得注意的

6 universe /ˈjuːnivəːs/ *n*. 宇宙

7 infinite /ˈinfinit/ *a*. 无限的，无穷的

8 expand /iksˈpænd/ *v*. 使……膨胀，扩张，伸展，展开

9 image /ˈimidʒ/ *n*. 图像，影像，肖像；外表，模样

10 majority /məˈdʒɔriti/ *n*. 多数，大多数

11 communication /kəˌmjuːniˈkeiʃən/ *n*. 沟通，交流，通信

12 benefit /ˈbenifit/ *n*. 利益；好处

13 continuously /kənˈtinjuəsli/ *ad*. 不断地，连续地

138

Lesson

36

The cost of government

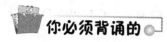
政府的开支

如果一个国家实际上处于分裂状态，使之联合起来就是政府的事情了。

凡是政府管理费用高的地方，用于发展国家经济的资金就会相应地减少。

如果企业中的每个人都在真诚地为提高企业利润而工作，那么企业的管理费用就会降低到相应的程度。

如果人民忠于职守，举止规矩，能受到政府的信赖，那么政府就不需要大批的警察和文职人员去促使人民遵纪守法。

如果一个国家处于分裂状态，政府不能相信人民的行动有利于国家，那么政府就不得不对人民进行监督、检查和控制。

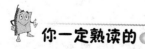
你一定熟读的

情景模拟对话一

A: We need to publish all the necessary information about management structure, guidelines and so on.

B: Yes, it should all be up on the company website by the end of the week.

A: Good. I just want everyone to be clear about where their division fits into the company structure.

B: What about that confusion as to whom the Project Managers would be reporting to? Has that been sorted out yet?

A: Yes, they'll be reporting to James Hu.

B: And do you still plan to meet with all the company managers to set out the new management guidelines?

A: Yes, I'm going to write to them all this week to give an outline of our new management practices.

B: Right, do you want me to help you draft that?

A: No, but I'll need you help in putting together my presentation.

B: And you and the board have agreed on the specifics.

A: Yes, we're going to be focusing on open management, horizontal management structures, and so on.

B: OK, well let me know when you need some input from me.

A: For now I'd prefer you to concentrate on sorting out all the details for the management training course.

B: We've selected the training company.

A: Oh good. How long is the course going to last?

B: It's going to be every Wednesday afternoon for two months.

A: And what made you choose them?

B: Well cost apart, they offer the most comprehensive package, they cover leadership, team and morale building and so on.

A: Will you be going along too?

B: Yes, I'm sure I'll learn something!

A: 我们需要公布有关的管理结构、指导方针等必要的资料。

B: 是的, 都应该在本周末前张贴在公司网站上。

A: 好, 我只希望每个人都了解自己的部门在整个公司的结构。

B: 那比较困惑的问题是, 项目经理要向谁作报告? 都整理出来了吗?

A: 是的，他们将向詹姆士胡报告。

B: 你是否计划与所有公司的管理人员开会，订出新的管理准则?

A: 是的，我要在这个星期给他们写出我们新的管理方法概要。

B: 是的，你要我帮你起草案吗?

A: 不用，但我需要你帮助我将我的发言整理到一起。

B: 你和董事会再具体商定。

A: 是的，我们将集中讨论开放式管理、横向管理结构等。

B: 好，那让我知道你什么时候需要这些?

A: 现在我希望你集中整理所有的管理培训课程的细节。

B: 我们已经选择了培训公司。

A: 哦，好的。课程要持续多长的时间?

B: 每个星期三的下午，会持续两个月。

A: 你为什么选择他们?

B: 除了费用外，他们提供最全面的方案，包括领导能力，团队建设等。

A: 你也会随同一起去吗?

B: 是的，我相信我会学到东西的!

情景模拟对话二

A: Hi, what's up?

B: The boss assigned me a great task to take Mr. Nash out to dinner this evening.

A: Oh, that company is one of our most important clients. I see why you're worried.

B: The boss said that I have to do a good job for entertaining him. If the guy is not satisfied the boss will fire me.

A: Is the boss going, too?

B: No. Everything will be easy for me if he is going. I was told that Nash is a heavy drinker and chain smoker. It's going to be hard keeping up with him.

A: You shouldn't try. If you drink too much, you might have trouble keeping the conversation going.

B: I'll have trouble in any case. That guy is interested in photographing and butterfly collecting, and wherever he is, he likes talking about that. I know nothing about the two things.

A: Why don't you take him to the Rose Restaurant? There are a lot of really beautiful hostesses and delicious food there.

B: I have thought of that, but the boss doesn't want to spend much money. He's such a well-known miser.

A: I guess you could pay half the bill out of your pocket.

B: I often end up doing that. I've spent as much as the boss has done entertaining clients.

A: 嗨，怎么了？

B: 我老板给我分配一个艰巨的任务，就是带着纳什先生今晚出去吃饭。

A: 喔，这个公司是你们很重要的客户，我知道为什么你担忧了。

B: 老板说必须让我把纳什先生服务周到了，如果他不满意的话，老板就会炒我鱿鱼。

A: 老板也去吗？

B: 不，如果他去了，我还好办。我听说纳什是一个喝酒很多而且不断抽烟的人。我想和他长时间呆在一起真的不容易。

A: 你不应该尝试，如果你喝多了的话，你们谈话都会费劲。

B: 我对任何事情都很发愁，这个人对摄影和收藏蝴蝶感兴趣，不管他在哪，他都喜欢谈论这些，而我对这两样什么都不知道。

A: 为什么不带他去蔷薇餐厅，那里有很漂亮的服务员，还有丰盛的食物。

B: 我也想过，但是老板不想花那么多钱，他可是典型的吝啬鬼。

A: 我猜一半的钱都是从你自己腰包拿吧。

B: 我经常最后这么做。我已经花了和老板款待客户一样多的钱。

你最好掌握的

1 management /ˈmænidʒmənt/ *n*. 管理，经营，处理

2 guideline /ˈɡaidlain/ *n*. 指引

3 website /ˈwebsait/ *n*. 网站

4 division /diˈviʒən/ *n*. 区分，分开，除法，公司，部门

5 confusion /kənˈfjuːʒən/ *n*. 混乱，混淆

6 sort /sɔːt/ *n*. 种类，样子 *v*. 分类，整理，排序

7 draft /drɑːft/ *n*. 草稿，草图；汇票 *v*. 起草，草拟；征募，征召

8 presentation /ˌprezenˈteiʃən/ *n*. 呈现；显示；外观；报告

9 specific /spiˈsifik/ *a*. 特殊的，明确的，具有特效的 *n*. 特效药，特性，详情

10 horizontal /ˌhɔriˈzɔntl/ *a*. 水平的，横的

11 input /ˈinput/ *n*. 输入

12 comprehensive /ˌkɔmpriˈhensiv/ *a*. 综合的，广泛的，理解的

13 select /siˈlekt/ *v*. 选择，挑选，选拔 *a*. 精选的；限制性的；选择严格的

14 morale /mɔˈrɑːl/ *n*. 士气，斗志

15 client /ˈklaiənt/ *n*. 顾客，委托人

16 chain smoke 一支一支不停地吸烟

17 miser /ˈmaizə/ *n*. 守财奴，吝啬鬼

18 hostess /ˈhəustis/ *n*. 女主人

Lesson

37 The process of ageing

 你必须背诵的

衰老过程

虽然在这个时期人的身材、体力和智力还有待发展和完善，但是在这个年龄死亡的可能性最小。

人类发现的最不愉快的一个事实是：人必然会衰老。

即使我们能避开战争、意外的事故和各种疾病，我们最终也会"老死"。

生命力随着时间流逝而丧失活力，人随着年龄的增长而接近死亡，这是不言而喻的。

我们通常看到的大多数动物，即使能让它们活得足够长久的话，也会像我们一样衰老的。

而我们人，在一定时间内是可以自行修复的，除了暴病而死或者意外事故外，至少足以克服一切一般疾病和事故。

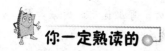

你一定熟读的

情景模拟对话一

A: Hello! Nice to see you again at the fitness centre. What exercises are you going to do today?

B: I'm going to do some jogging on the treadmill.

A: Good idea. I'd suggest you do some crunches too. They're great for getting in shape. Make sure you do them correctly.

B: OK. I will. Could you help me with the treadmill? I found it difficult to get the setting right last time.

A: Sure. Is today only your second visit?

B: Yes，it is. I'll be coming here regularly. I think I need regular exercise to get in shape and then to stay in shape.

A: The treadmill is excellent for helping you to build up stamina. Each time you use it，increase this distance. Don't worry about your speed at first. You can increase that later.

B: I was told not to put too much pressure on my body at first. I need to build up slowly.

A: That's right. You don't want to injure yourself by exercising too much or in the wrong way.

A: 你好，很高兴又在健身中心和你见面了？你今天做什么训练呀？

B: 我想在跑步机上做些慢跑。

A: 好主意。我建议你也要做些仰卧起坐，这对你的体形有很大好处，保证你做它们没错。

B: 好的。你能帮帮我弄一下这个跑步机吗？上一次我发现设置正确的时间很难。

A: 好，这只是你第二次来吗？

B: 是的，我会经常来这里。我想我需要有规律的来锻炼我的体形，并且能保持住。

A: 跑步机能极好地帮助你增强你的精力，每次你用的时候，就增加距离。第一次不要担心速度，过后你可以增加的。

B: 别人告诉我第一次不要对自己的身体施加太多压力，我需要慢慢的来。

A: 没错，过度锻炼以及用错误的方法锻炼会损害你的身体。

情景模拟对话二

A: Good afternoon，Madam. How can I help you?

B: Well，I am a bit out of shape. I'm thinking about exercising to keep fit.

A: Oh，that's good news for us.

B: So what do you provide?

A: First of all，we'll design a custom-made work-out plan according to your habits.

B: How can you get that done?

A: Well，you have a qualified personal trainer assigned to you. He will give you a fitness assessment and then come up with the work-out plan for your needs.

B: What else?

A: Since everyone is different，your personal trainer will find you suitable exercise equipment and teach you all the techniques to help you achieve your fitness level and goals.

B: Sounds pretty good. How much does it cost?

A: That depends. We offer memberships for one month，half a year and one year.

B: Maybe I'll do one month. Just have a try first — not too tough at the beginning.

A: Wise decision. You'll find it's totally worth it.

B: What are your business hours?

A: We are open from 6 am to midnight. You are welcome anytime.

B: Thank you.

A: 下午好，女士。有什么能为您效劳的吗？

B: 那个，我身体有点走形了，我在考虑做点运动来保持体形。

A: 哦，这对我们是好消息啊。

B: 你们能提供什么（服务)？

A: 首先，我们会根据顾客的兴趣为顾客做一个健身计划。

B: 你们会怎么做呢？

A: 哦，我们会为每一个顾客安排一名专业的私人健身教练。他会给你做一份健身评估，然后根据需求制定出相应的健身计划。

B: 还有别的吗？

A: 因为每个人的情况不同，所以私人教练会帮你找合适的运动器材，教你具体的使用方法以帮你达到健身的目标。

B: 听起来很不错。怎么收费呢？

A: 看情况的。我们提供一个月、半年和一年的会员卡。

B: 我要一个月的。先试一下。开始先别太多了。

A: 很聪明的决定。你会发现它很超值的。

B: 你们的营业时间是什么？

A: 我们从早上 6 点一直开到晚上 12 点。随时欢迎您的光临。

B: 谢谢。

 你最好掌握的

1 fitness /ˈfitnis/ n. 健康；适当

2 jog /dʒɔg/ v. 轻推，慢跑 n. 轻敲，慢跑

3 treadmill /ˈtredmil/ n. 踏车，单调乏味的工作，跑步机

4 crunch /krʌntʃ/ n. 嘎吱的响声；仰卧起坐 v. 嘎吱作响

5 stamina /ˈstæminə/ n. 精力，活力

6 excellent /ˈeksələnt/ a. 极好的，优秀的

7 keep fit 保持健康

8 custom-made /ˈkʌstəmˈmeid/ a. 定做的

9 qualify /'kwɔlifai/ v. 取得资格；限定，修饰

10 assign /ə'sain/ v. 分配，指派

11 assessment /ə'sesmənt/ n. 估价，评估

12 equipment /i'kwipmənt/ n. 设备，装备

13 technique /tek'ni:k/ n. 技术

14 that depends 视情况而定

15 pretty /'priti/ a. 漂亮的 ad. 相当地

Lesson

38

Water and the traveler

你必须背诵的

水和旅行者

即使管道供水系统在水源处是安全的，等水到达龙头时就不一定总是安全的了。

短途旅行到水质不保险的地区时，旅游者应该避免饮用水龙头的水或未经处理的任何其他来源的水。

可以把饮料置于冰块之上来冷却，而不是把冰块加进饮料之中。

酒精可用作医学上的消毒剂，但决不可用来消毒饮用水。

那些计划去偏远地区旅行、或者没有现成饮用水的国家居住的人，应该知道如何使水适用于饮用的各种办法。

你一定熟读的

情景模拟对话一

A: This is how a holiday should be, relaxing on the beach with a nice cool drink.

B: Isn't it wonderful here? The kids are enjoying themselves in the swimming pool. I hope it's safe.

A: Don't worry about them. They're very responsible. Besides, there are many people and there's lifeguard employed by the hotel. Waiter! Could I have another drink? Thank you. So, what shall we do this evening?

B: The kids said that they wanted to go to a party at the hotel. There's a special one just for kids.

A: So, we could try the restaurant that was recommended in the guidebook. Then we could go to a club. We haven't been to one for ages.

B: That's a great idea. We can really enjoy ourselves without worrying about the kids.

A: Now, how about going for a swim in the sea? We shouldn't sunbathe all day.

A: 这才是过假期的样子，舒适地躺在沙滩上，伴着一杯凉饮。

B: 这很棒吧？孩子们在游泳池玩，我希望那能很安全。

A: 不要担心他们。他们很负责任的。再说了，这有很多人，而且宾馆也雇了救生员。服务生，能不能给我换一杯饮料？谢谢，那么我们晚上做什么呢？

B: 孩子们说他们想参加酒店的派对。这正好有一个专门为孩子们设计的派对。

A: 我们应该尝试着看看在旅行指南上介绍的餐厅，然后我们可以去餐厅，要知道我们有好多年没去了。

B: 好主意，这下我们可以真正地享受不顾及孩子们的快乐时光了。

A: 现在我们去海里游泳怎么样？我们不能整天都晒太阳浴。

情景模拟对话二

A: Where do you think we should go on holiday this summer?

B: I'd like to go to Australia. I know it's far to go, but I think it would be something different and special.

A: I'd really like to go to the Caribbean. We can relax on the beached and enjoy the sunshine.

B: There are beaches in Australia too, but I would prefer a more active holiday this year. We could visit Ayers Rock and The Great Barrier Reef. It would be so exciting.

A: But would it be relaxing? In summer, I'll be quite tired from doing so much work. The last thing I need is to use more energy racing around Australia. I'd need another holiday to recover!

B: Oh, come on! A tour of Australia would be relaxing because you'd be doing something different and not working.

A: Do you think so? I'm not so sure. Anyway, tell me your plans for an Australian holiday. How long do you think we should spend there?

B: I think we should go for two weeks. We could spend a week in the bush and a week at The Great Barrier Reef — including a few days on the beach.

A: That doesn't sound too bad. I'd certainly like to go diving. That's one reason I wanted to go to the Caribbean.

B: We could hire a car and travel around the interior of Australia for several days. If we hire a car, we can go where we like.

A: We'd have to plan our drive before we leave. Let's get a good guidebook form the bookstore when we go shopping tomorrow.

B: It looks like I might have convinced you to go to Australia!

A: 我们这个暑假要去哪里过假期?

B: 我想去澳大利亚,我知道很远,但是我想这一定会很与众不同的。

A: 我想去加勒比海,我们可以在沙滩上放松,享受阳光。

B: 澳大利亚也有很多海滩呀,但是我更期待一个活跃的假期。我们可以去艾尔斯山还有大堡礁,一定会很刺激。

A: 但是这样能放松吗? 在夏天做太多的工作我会很劳累的。最后我最需要做的就是攒足体力来环游澳大利亚。我还需要另外一个假期来恢复。

B: 哦,别这样,澳大利亚之旅就会让你放松,你可以做除了工作以外的不同的事情。

A: 你这样认为？我可不这么想。不管怎么样，告诉我你的澳大利亚之旅的计划。我们会在那多久？

B: 我想有两个星期吧，一个星期在丛林，另一个星期在大堡礁，当然还包括几天在沙滩的享受。

A: 听起来也不错嘛。我真的好想去潜水，这也是我为什么想去加勒比海的原因。

B: 我们也可以租辆车，在澳大利亚国内玩几天。如果我们能租到车，我们就可以去任何我们想去的地方了。

A: 在我们离开之前要计划好我们的行程。我们明天逛街的时候从书店买一本好点的旅游指南吧。

B: 看样子我好像说服了你去澳大利亚呢。

 你最好掌握的

1 recommend /rekə'mend/ v. 建议，推荐，劝告，介绍

2 sunbathe /'sʌnbeið/ n. 日光浴

3 recover /ri'kʌvə/ v. 恢复，复原，补偿

4 interior /in'tiəriə/ a. 内部的，内地的，国内的 n. 内部，内地

5 hire /'haiə/ v. 雇请，出租 n. 租金，租用，雇用

6 guidebook /'gaidbuk/ n. 旅行指南

Lesson

39

What every writer wants

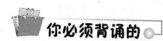

作家之所需

凡是我所认识和尊敬的作家，都坦率地承认在他们动笔的时候，不清楚要写什么，怎么写。

我从未听说过任何一位作家像我们在学校学的那样，动笔前先列什么提纲。

作家在剪裁修改、构思时间、穿插情节、甚至从头重写的过程中，会领悟到素材中有很多东西是他刚动笔时所未意识到的。

初稿是才华，以后各稿是艺术。

一旦作家从内心的紊乱中理出头绪，就应按任何评论家想象不到的无情规范约束自己去写作。

当他沽名钓誉时，他就脱离了自我生活，脱离了对自己灵魂最深处世界的探索。

你一定熟读的

情景模拟对话一

A: Hi, Charlie! What are you reading?

B: Hi, Bob. I'm reading a biography.

A: Who's it about?

B: It's about Bob Dylan.

A: Who is he?

B: He's a famous American musician.

A: Who's the author?

B: It was written by Howard.

A: What do you think about it?

B: It's great! I've learned a lot from reading it.

A: Can I read it when you're done?

B: Sure, Bob! I'm on chapter 12 now, so I'm almost finished.

A: How many chapters does the book have?

B: There are 15 chapters in total.

A: When do you think you'll have finished reading it?

B: I should be done by Friday. I'll give it to you in class then.

A: Thanks, Charlie!

B: No problem, Bob.

A: 嗨，查理！你在读什么？

B: 嗨，鲍伯！我在看自传。

A: 关于谁的？

B: 是关于鲍伯·迪伦的。

A: 他是谁？

B: 他是美国著名的音乐家。

A: 那作者是谁？

B: 是霍华德写的。

A: 你怎么看这个呢？

B: 很棒呢！通过读这本书我学到了很多。

A: 你读完之后我能看看吗？

B: 当然，鲍伯！我现在看到12章了，我快看完了。

A: 这本书一共有多少章？

B: 总共有15章。

A: 你什么时候能读完？

B: 星期五能看完。我会在课堂上给你的。

A: 谢谢了，查理。

B: 没问题的，鲍伯。

情景模拟对话二

A: I can't believe my English teacher is making me read *pride and prejudice*!

B: Why not? It's a classic, in fact, it's one of my favorite novels.

A: But it's so old.

B: Don't judge a book by its cover. Do you know what it's about?

A: No, not at all.

B: First of all, it's a romance novel, set in the early 19th century.

A: I didn't realize it was a romance novel. What's the main storyline?

B: It's basically about a mother who tried to marry off all of her five girls.

A: Why does she want to do that?

B: Since she doesn't have a son, she hopes that one of the girls will marry a wealthy man. That way, all of his daughters will be cared for.

A: Won't they get her inheritance?

B: No, that's the problem. Though they are well-off, once she dies, her house will go to her cousin. So, the girls will have nothing.

A: I see. This sounds interesting! Maybe my teacher isn't so horrible after all.

B: So, are you going to read the novel or the movie?

A: There's movie? My teacher didn't tell me that!

新概念英语4地道口语步步为赢

B: That's probably because she wants you to read the book first.

A: It would take a lot of time.

B: How about this? When you finish the book, I'll get the movie and watch it with you.

A: OK. That sounds like a deal.

A: 我真不敢相信我的英语老师让我读《傲慢与偏见》。

B: 为什么不能呢? 这部小说很经典的。事实上,这是我最喜欢的小说之一。

A: 但是它好旧啊。

B: 不要根据它的封面来判断好不好。你知道这是讲什么的吗?

A: 一点也不知道。

B: 首先,这是一部浪漫的小说,创作在19世纪早期。

A: 我不认为这是一部浪漫小说。主要的故事情节是什么?

B: 主要是讲关于一个母亲想要嫁掉她所有的5个女儿。

A: 她为什么想这样做?

B: 因为她没有儿子,她希望其中的一个女儿能嫁给一个有钱人,这样她所有的女儿就都会被宠爱了。

A: 她们不能得到她的财产吗?

B: 不,这不是问题,尽管他们生活算是富裕,但是一旦她去世了,她的房子就会归她的表亲,所以,女儿们什么都得不到。

A: 听起来挺有趣的。可能我的老师根本没那么可怕。

B: 所以,你会读小说或者看电影吗?

A: 有电影吗? 老师都没告诉我。

B: 那可能是因为她想先让你读书吧。

A: 这会花费很多时间的。

B: 这样好不好,如果你看完小说,我会和你一起看这个电影的。

A: 好的,听起来像个交易。

你最好掌握的

1 musician /mjuːˈzɪʃən/ n. 音乐家

2 chapter /'tʃæptə/ *n*. 章，回，篇

3 prejudice /'predʒudis/ *n*. 偏见，成见 *v*. 使……存偏见，使……有成见，伤害

4 classic /'klæsik/ *a*. 第一流的，最优秀的，古典的 *n*. 古典作品，杰作

5 storyline /'stɔːrilain/ *n*. 故事情节

6 romance /rə'mæns,rəu-/ *n*. 冒险故事，浪漫史，传奇文学

7 marry off 把女儿嫁出去

8 inheritance /in'heritəns/ *n*. 遗传，遗产

9 horrible /'hɔrəbl/ *a*. 可怕的，令人毛骨悚然的，令人讨厌的

10 well-off /'wel'ɔf/ *a*. 顺利的；富有的；繁荣昌盛的

Lesson

40

Waves

 你必须背诵的

海 浪

海洋是大海和空气相斗的产物，一种象征永恒的生物体现。

阳光使空气开始流动，产生节奏，获得生命。

如果水和浪一起移动的话，那么大海和海里所有的东西就会向岸边疾涌而来，带来明显的灾难性后果。

公海上起伏的波浪是由 3 个自然因素构成的：风，地球的运动或震颤和月亮、太阳的引力。

一旦波浪形成，地球引力是持续不断企图使海面复原为平面的力量。

 你一定熟读的

情景模拟对话一

A: Hi! Good morning, everybody! I will be your dragoman（tour guide）for your trip in Guilin.

B: It seems there are so many beautiful sceneries in Guilin. What are we going to see first?

A: Today we are going to visit Elephant Trunk Hill.

B: Elephant Trunk hill? Sounds interesting.

A: Right, as its name suggests, the hill looks like a giant elephant drinking water with its trunk in the Li River.

B: Are we going to take the Li River boat ride today?

A: No. Tomorrow we will because the boat ride is a one day trip.

B: Oh, I can't wait to take the boat ride. There is a saying that goes like this "Guilin boasts the most beautiful scenery under Heaven."

A: You are absolutely right. Seeing is believing. You will see it tomorrow. OK, let's go to the Elephant Trunk hill first.

B: OK. Let's go.

A: Here we are. Look! That is Elephant Trunk hill. You can see that between the trunk and the legs there is a moon-shaped cave.

B: I see halfway up the hill there is a cave which goes through the hill. Does that serve as the eyes of the elephant?

A: Yes. That is the eye of the elephant. On top of the hill stands a pagoda named Puxian Pagoda, built in the Ming Dynasty (1368-1644).

B: Could you do me a favor?

A: Sure.

B: Could you take a picture for me?

A: OK. S-m-i-l-e!

B: Thank you so much.

A: You are welcome. Let's go to our next scenery Reed Flute Cave.

A: 嗨，大家早上好，我是你们这次桂林之旅的导游。

B: 看起来桂林有好多漂亮的风景，我们先要看什么呢？

A: 今天我们去参观象鼻山。

B: 象鼻山？听起来挺有趣的。

A: 对，顾名思义，这座山，看起来就像一只巨大的大象在用它的鼻子在漓江饮水一样。

B: 我们今天是乘船去漓江吗？

A: 不，明天我们乘船，因为乘船是一天的旅行。

B: 哦，真是迫不及待地想坐船，不是有一句古话说："桂林山水甲天下"嘛。

A: 完全正确。眼见为实，明天你就会看到了。好了，让我们先去象鼻山吧。

B: 好，出发吧。

A: 我们到了。看，这就是象鼻山。你可以看到在它的鼻子和腿之间有一个月亮形状的洞。

B: 我在这座山的半山腰看见一个洞，它是穿过这座山的。这就作为大象的眼睛吧？

A: 对，那是大象的眼睛。在山的顶部树立着一个宝塔，叫做蒲仙塔，建立于明代（1368～1644 年）。

B: 能帮我一个忙吗？

A: 可以。

B: 帮我照一张照片吧。

A: 好。笑一个。

B: 非常感谢。

A: 不客气，现在我们去下一个景点，芦笛岩。

情景模拟对话二

A: This place serves good breakfasts, don't you think?

B: Yes. But I'm not used to eating American-style breakfast.

A: What are you planning to do today?

B: I saw yesterday that they rent windsurfers at the beach. I want to rent one.

A: Have you done windsurfing before?

B: No, but it looks fun. I always wanted to try it.

A: Can you take a little advice from a friend?

B: Sure. What?

A: Don't waste your money. Windsurfing is very hard. And it will be windy today. They will charge you fifty dollars for a half hour, and you won't be able to windsurf. You will fall and fall and fall.

B: But I always wanted to try it.

A: Yes，but it takes a long time to learn. You would spend a thousand dollars to learn it on a rental windsurfer.

B: Well，I will see. How was your day at the office?

A: Hectic. It's always hectic. But how was your windsurfing?

B: I tried it for a half-hour. It was interesting, but... well... I couldn't really do it.

A: See? I told you. It's very hard.

B: I couldn't even stand on it and hold the sail. I probably fell down fifty times.

A: Fifty times?

B: Yes，it was really stupid.

A: And how much did it cost to rent it?

B: It was fifty dollars for a half-hour.

A: Well，that's not too bad then.

B: What do you mean? It's expensive!

A: Yes，but you have to calculate a little. You paid fifty dollars and you fell down fifty times. So you only spent one dollar per fall. That's cheap.

A: 这家的早餐不错吧?

B: 不错，但是我还是不习惯美国的早餐。

A: 你今天打算做什么?

B: 昨天我在海边看到有人租冲浪板，我想租一个。

A: 你以前冲过浪吗?

B: 没有，但是看起来很好玩，我一直想试试看。

A: 你可以听听朋友的意见吗?

B: 当然，请说。

A: 别浪费钱了，冲浪很困难的，而且今天风很大。他们半小时收费 50 美元，你根本冲不起来。你会一直落水的。

B: 但是我一直想试试看。

A: 不过学这个要很久。你租冲浪板来学会让你花上 1000 美元。

B: 我再看看。今天工作得如何?

A: 忙啊，一直很忙。你有去冲浪吗？

B: 我冲了半小时。挺有趣的，但是我真的不太会。

A: 看吧！我告诉过你很困难的。

B: 我甚至站不上去，也抓不到帆，我大概落水 50 次。

A: 50 次？

B: 对啊，真笨。

A: 你租它花了多少钱？

B: 半小时 50 美元。

A: 那还不算糟嘛。

B: 你说什么？很贵的！

A: 没错，不过你算算看。你花了 50 元，摔了 50 次。所以摔一次只花了 1 美元，很便宜啊。

 你最好掌握的

1 giant /ˈdʒaiənt/ a. 巨大的 n. 巨人

2 scenery /ˈsiːnəri/ n. 风景

3 absolutely /ˈæbsəluːtli/ ad. 绝对地，完全地；独立地；确实地

4 serve /səːv/ v. 可作……用，服务，对待

5 pagoda /pəˈɡəudə/ n. 宝塔，塔

6 windsurfer /ˈwindˌsəːfə/ n. 滑浪帆板

7 hectic /ˈhektik/ a. 兴奋的，繁忙的

8 calculate /ˈkælkjuleit/ v. 计算，估计，打算

Lesson

41

Training elephants

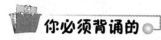 你必须背诵的

训练大象

训象有两种主要的方法，我们分别称之为强硬法和温柔法。

温柔法要求在最初阶段保持较大的耐心，但这种方法可以训练出性情愉快，脾气温顺，能忠实为人服务多年的大象。

大象和狗一样，喜欢有一个专一的主人，而且会对主人产生相当深厚的私人感情。

下一步就是把象带到训练场所，这是一件棘手的事，需要在它两侧拴上两头驯服的大象帮忙才能完成。

两位助手骑在驯服的象的背上，从两侧控制新捕的象，其他人唱着单调舒缓的歌声用手抚摸象的皮肤。

 你一定熟读的

情景模拟对话

A: What would we do after work?

B: How about going to see a movie?

A: It's a good idea, but I don't want to see movie today, how about going to zoo today?

B: But it is too night to go there, it is fifteen past seven already, is the zoo closed when we arrive?

A: I am not sure, but I think it won't close so early.

B: Why risk discovery? I won't risk an action until we are sure of the zoo's condition. I prefer watching movie to going to zoo.

A: OK! As you wish.

A: 我们下班后，做什么好？

B: 不如去看电影吧？

A: 不错的建议，但我今天不想看电影，不如去动物园。

B: 现在已经7点15分了，太晚了吧，等我们到那，动物园都关门了吧？

A: 我不知道，但我想不会那么早关门。

B: 为什么要冒这个险，我不想在没弄清楚真实的情况下去做这件事，我更倾向于看电影。

A: 好吧，就听你的。

口语拓展

We often say that animals are our best friends. However, in real life, we human beings are often very selfish. Sometimes, we often betray this friendship by torturing and even sacrificing the lives of our "friends" for certain selfish reasons. Vivisection, or animal testing, is one of the selfish behaviors that we frequently show.

Animals have feelings, thoughts and dignity like men. Both scientific researches and life experience have long proved these to us. A knife cut on any part of our body would incur sharp pain. Facing death that is imposed on us, we would be terrified out of our wits. When have we ever realized that animals have the same feeling as they are treated the same way?

We can not change the past. We only have the present and the future. What is gone is gone, including those animals that had suffered great pains and even sacrificed their precious lives for the scientific and technological progress of mankind. However, we should bear in mind that while we are thinking about our own benefits, we should also have other animals in mind.

　　我们常说动物是人类最好的朋友，然而，现实中，我们人类却往往表现得非常自私，常为一己之利而去出卖、折磨、甚至牺牲自己"朋友"的生命。动物试验便是我们这种自私行为的表现之一。

　　动物和我们人类一样是有感觉、有思想、有尊严的。无论是科学研究还是生活经验都早已向我们证实了这一点。刀割破了我们身上的任何一个地方，我们会感到剧烈的疼痛；面对强加于我们的死亡，我们会感到惊恐万状。什么时候我们才能认识到当我们这样对待其他动物时，它们也是同样的感觉呢？

　　我们无法改变过去，我们只拥有现在和将来。过去的已经过去了，包括那些为人类科技进步而遭受了无尽痛苦甚至牺牲了宝贵生命的动物们。我们需要谨记的一点是：当我们在考虑人类自身利益的时候，也替其他动物们想一想。

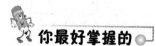 你最好掌握的

1 discovery /dis'kʌvəri/ *n*. 发现，发现物

2 selfish /'selfiʃ/ *a*. 自私的，利己的

3 betray /'betrei/ 出卖，背叛

4 torture /'tɔːtʃə/ *v*. 拷问，折磨 *n*. 拷问，痛苦

5 sacrifice /'sækrifais/ *v*. 牺牲，祭祀 *n*. 牺牲，供俸，祭品

6 vivisection /ˌvivi'sekʃən/ *n*. 动物解剖实验

7 dignity /'digniti/ *n*. 尊严，庄严，高尚，端庄

8 impose /im'pəuz/ *v*. 加上，强迫，征收（税款）；利用，欺骗

9 wit /wit/ *n*. 智力，才智

10 incur /in'kəː/ *v*. 招致，蒙受，遭遇

11 terrified /'terifaid/ *a*. 恐惧的，受惊吓的

12 suffer /'sʌfə/ *v*. 遭受，忍受；忍受

Lesson

42

Recording an earthquake

 你必须背诵的

记录地震

如果地震轻微，只有不稳定的木棒倒下；如果地震剧烈，所有的木棒都会倒下。

理想的目标是设计出这样一种仪器：当地震发生时，它能用笔在纸上记录下大地和桌子的运动情况。

由于纸在笔尖下来回运动，纸的表面就会用墨水记录下来地板运动的情况。

如果把这种仪器安装在距震源 700 多英里远的地方，曲线记录就能显示出前后相间的这 3 种地震波。

 你一定熟读的

情景模拟对话

A: Do you know what happened on May 12th this year?

B: Of course, I think people all over the world should know this matter — a deadly earthquake.

A: I think so. A magnitude 8.0 earthquake happened in Wenchuan,

Sichuan province. It is the worst earthquake which happened in China since the founding of New China.

B: Yes. A lot of people lost their lives in this disater. Meanwhile, many people lost their homes and families.

A: What a pity! Fortunately, people from all over the country try their best to help them. They donate money to the quake-hit areas and donate something useful to them, such as food, water, books, clothes, quilts and so on. I also donate my pocket money to them.

B: Oh, me too. Besides, I donated several new books to them. I hope that children can read these books to forget the sadness.

A: Moreover, the government decided that the days from 19th to 21st on May were mourning acorss China for the victims of Wenchuan earthquake.

B: All people showed respect to the victims those days.

A: I hope the victims don't lose heart.

B: In my opinion, they won't lose heart. With the help of the people in China and with the leadership of the Party, the victims will overcome all difficulties to rebuild their homes.

A: 你知道今年 5 月 12 日发生什么了吗？

B: 当然，我想全世界的人都知道这个事情，一场致命的地震。

A: 我也是这么想的。在四川汶川里氏 8.0 级的巨大地震，这也是新中国成立以来最严重的一次地震了。

B: 是，好多人在这场灾难中都失去了生命，还有好多人失去了家人和家园。

A: 真的很不幸，幸运的是，全国各个地方的人们都努力帮助他们，他们捐钱、捐物给受灾地区，如食物、水、书、衣服、被子等。我也把我的零用钱捐出去了。

B: 我也是，而且，我还捐了一些新书，我希望孩子们能够读这些书，来忘记他们的悲伤。

A: 政府也决定，5 月的 19~21 日作为全中国默哀四川地震受难者的日子。

B: 所有的人都对受难者表示了由衷的尊重。

A: 我希望受难者们不要失去勇气。

B: 在我看来，他们不会的，有中国人民和中国共产党的帮助，
受难者们一定会克服困难，重建家园的。

口语拓展

In the past hundred years, there have been frequent natural disasters, such as floods, droughts, mud-rock flows, seismic sea waves, earthquakes, windstorms and the stretching of new deserts. The disasters have killed millions upon millions of people, destroyed countless homes, and wiped out numerous pieces of fertile land.

Now more and more people become aware that those disasters have much to do with what we have done to the earth. We have cut down too many trees in the forests, we have badly polluted the environment, and we have shocked our own home-planet time and again with tremendously powerful explosions of nuclear bombs. As a result, climates have become abnormal, rainwater rushes down hillsides angrily, and the underground energy goes up to revenge itself on us.

The earth is our only home-planet. It is urgent for us to stop damaging it, and to do our best to protect it and make it a lovely place suitable to live in, for we have nowhere to go.

在过去的 100 年里，经常性的发生自然灾害，如洪水、干旱、泥石流、海洋地震波、地震、风暴和已经不断延伸的沙漠。这些灾难使得数以百万的人失去了生命，摧毁了无数的家园，吞噬了无数肥沃的土地。

现在越来越多的人开始意识到，这些灾难与我们对地球所做的事情有个很大的关系。我们在森林里砍伐很多树木，严重破坏我们的环境，我们一次又一次地用原子弹去轰炸我们地球家园。结果，环境变的不正常起来，雨水愤怒地冲垮了山腰，地下能量冲出地面对我们实行报复。

地球是我们唯一的家园。我们必须马上停止去破坏它，然后尽力去保护它，使之成为一个适合生存的令人愉悦的地方，因为我们没有地方去。

你最好掌握的

1. deadly /ˈdedli/ a. 致命的，致死的；极端的，非常的
2. magnitude /ˈmægnitjuːd/ n. 巨大，重要
3. donate /dəuˈneit/ v. 捐赠
4. quake-hit /kweik-hit/ a. 受地震袭击的
5. mourn /mɔːn/ v. 哀悼，哀痛
6. overcome /ˌəuvəˈkʌm/ v. 战胜，克服
7. frequent /ˈfriːkwənt/ a. 经常的，频繁的 vt. 常到，常去
8. stretch /stretʃ/ v. 伸展，张开，延伸 n. 伸展，张开；一段时间，一段路程
9. seismic /ˈsaizmik/ a. 地震的
10. countless /ˈkaʊtlis/ a. 无数的
11. wipe out 根除，消灭
12. numerous /ˈnjuːmərəs/ a. 为数众多的，许多的
13. fertile /ˈfəːtail; ˈfəːtil/ a. 肥沃的，多产的，富饶的
14. tremendously /triˈmendəsli/ ad. 惊人地
15. shock /ʃɔk/ v. 使震惊 n. 震动，打击，震惊
16. revenge /riˈvendʒ/ v. 报仇，报复 n. 报仇，复仇，报复
17. urgent /ˈəːdʒənt/ a. 急迫的，紧要的，紧急的

Are there strangers in space?

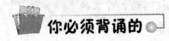
你必须背诵的

宇宙中有外星人吗？

如果设想有一颗行星和我们地球的情况基本相似，那几乎肯定会产生生命。

太阳系的其他行星的温度都接近绝对零度，并围绕着以氢气为主的大气层。

他们可能在几千年前或几百万年前已来过我们的地球，并且发现我们地球当时普遍存在着的原始状态同他们先进的知识相比是索然无味的。

这种自动化信息装置，在接收到我们的无线电和电视信号后，完全有可能把这些信号发回到原来的行星。

没有这种手段，要想寻觅其他星球上的智力生命，就如同去伦敦见一位朋友，事先未约定地点，而荒唐地在街上游逛，以期碰巧遇上一样。

你一定熟读的

情景模拟对话

A: Do you believe in UFOs?

B: Of course, they are out there.

A: But I never saw them.

B: Are you stupid? They are called UFOs, so not everybody can see them.

A: You mean that you can them.

B: That's right. I can see them in my dreams.

A: They come to the earth?

B: No. Their task is to send the aliens here from the outer space.

A: Aliens from the outer space? Do you talk to them? What do they look like?

B: OK, OK, one by one, please! They look like robots, but they can speak. Their mission is to make friends with human beings.

A: That means that you talk to them? In which language?

B: Of course in English, they learn English on Mars too.

A: Wow. Sounds fantastic!

A: 你相信有不明飞行物吗?

B: 当然了, 它们就在那儿呢。

A: 但是我从来就没有看见过啊。

B: 你笨吧你, 它们叫做不明飞行物, 所以不是每个人都能看到的啊。

A: 那你的意思就是说你能看见。

B: 对啊, 我在梦中看到它们。

A: 它们要到我们地球上来吗?

B: 不是。它们的任务是把外星人从太空送到地球上来。

A: 从外太空来的外星人吗? 那你和它们说话了吗? 它们都长什么样子啊?

B: 好, 好, 打住, 一个一个问好吗? 它们看起来就像是机器人,但是它们会说话，它们的使命就是和我们地球人做朋友。
A: 那就是说你们对话了？用哪种语言呢？
B: 当然是用英语，它们在火星上也学英语的。
A: 哇噻！听起来太不可思议了。

口语拓展

Some people believe that the Mars could support life in the future if the right conditions were produced. The first step would be to warm the planet using certain gases which trap the Sun's heat in the planet's atmosphere. With warmth, water and carbon dioxide, simple plants could begin to grow. These plants could slowly make the Mars more suitable for living. It is estimated that the whole process might take between 100,000 and 200,000 years. In the meantime, people could begin to live on the planet in special closed environments. They would provide a lot of useful information about conditions on the Mars and the problems connected with living there.

一些人相信在将来如果条件可以的话，火星上是可以生存的。第一步就是利用某些气体来温暖这个行星，而这个气体要吸收太阳在地球的大气层中的热量。伴随着温暖、水和二氧化碳，简单的植物可以开始生长。这些植物可以慢慢使火星更适合人类居住。据估计，整个过程可能要花费10万～20万年。在此期间，人们开始能够在行星的特殊的封闭的环境生活。他们会提供很多有用的信息，有关在火星上生活的情况及在火星上存在的问题。

你最好掌握的

1 mission /ˈmiʃən/ n. 任务，代表团，使命
2 dioxide /daiˈɔksaid/ n. 二氧化物
3 estimate /ˈestimeit/ v. 估计，估价，评价 n. 估计，估价

Lesson

44

Patterns of culture

文化的模式

最重要的是，风俗在实践中和信仰上所起的举足轻重的作用，以及它所表现出来的极其丰富多彩的形式。

人们所看到的是一个受特定的风俗习惯、制度和思想方式剪辑过的世界。

直到我们理解了风俗的规律性和多样性，我们才能明白人类生活中主要的复杂现象。

只有在某些基本的主张被接受下来，同时有些主张被激烈反对的时候，对风俗的研究才是全面的，才会有收获。

我们首先需要达到这样一种成熟的程度：不用自己的信仰去反对我们邻居的迷信。

你一定熟读的

情景模拟对话一

A: There seems to be so much christmas history.

B: I know. I don't know how I will ever remember all of it.

A: I suppose it is because it has such a long history.

B: It's interesting to see how the culture of christmas has changed over the year.

A: And I suppose that it will continue to change.

B: Do you think that our children will celebrate christmas differently than we do?

A: Possibly. I know one thing for sure.

B: What's that?

A: Our children will want more expensive gifts than we got!

A: 看起来圣诞节的历史很多。

B: 我知道。我不知道我怎样才能记住所有的历史。

A: 我觉得这是因为它的历史源远流长的缘故。

B: 看到圣诞节文化如何随着时光的推移而发生改变很有趣。

A: 而且我觉得它还会继续发生变化。

B: 你认为我们的孩子和我们庆祝圣诞节的方式会不一样吗？

A: 可能吧。我对一件事很确定。

B: 那是什么？

A: 我们的孩子想要的礼物比我们要的会更昂贵！

情景模拟对话二

A: Is everything ready for the Christmas party?

B: Almost. We've decorated the Christmas tree with plenty of tinsel and baubles.

A: Wonderful! I'll put the presents under the tree later, how's the food?

B: I've prepared most and we've got plenty of snack foods, you know, crisps, biscuits, and so on. Are you going to make the punch?

A: Yes. I've bought all the things to go in it. It won't take long to make. How many people are coming to the party?

B: I think everyone will be coming. Dave doesn't come because he has to go to his parent's home and they live in Scotland.

A: Do we have Christmas pudding?

B: Yes，we do. I hope we have enough for everyone. Did you send out all your Christmas cards in time?

A: Yes，I did. I send most of them a week ago. I've brought some with me to the party to give to people in person.

B: I did the same. I spent hours yesterday evening wrapping presents. I hope I didn't forget to buy anyone something!

A: I hope you didn't forget mine!

A: 圣诞晚会的东西都准备好了吗？

B: 差不多了，我们已经把圣诞树装点了金光闪闪的小饰品。

A: 好棒呀！我一会就把礼物放在树的下面，吃的准备得怎么样了？

B: 我准备了好多。我们也准备了一些小吃，像薯片、饼干等，你要做鸡尾酒吗？

A: 我已经准备了所有的东西。不会浪费很长时间的，今天晚会上会来多少人？

B: 我想每个人都会来。戴夫不会来了，因为他必须去他的父母那里，他们住苏格兰。

A: 我们准备圣诞布丁了吗？

B: 准备了，而且也足够了。你及时发送圣诞贺卡了吗？

A: 是的，我一周前就发了。晚会上我自己也买了一些，然后再亲自给出去。

B: 我也一样，我昨天整晚都在打包装，我希望我没有忘记买任何东西！

A: 我希望你没有忘记我的。

你最好掌握的

1 suppose /sə'pəuz/ v. 推想，假设，以为，认为

2 tinsel /ˈtinsəl/ *n*. 闪亮的金属片 *v*. 用金箔装饰 *a*. 闪亮的，华而不实的

3 bauble /ˈbɔːbl/ *n*. 美观而无价值的饰物

4 snack /snæk/ *n*. 小吃，点心

5 pudding /ˈpudiŋ/ *n*. 布丁

6 wrap /ræp/ *v*. 覆盖，包围，裹，包 *n*. 披肩，围巾

Lesson

45

Of men and galaxies

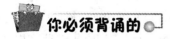 你必须背诵的

人和星系

我断定，如果没有现代化的武器，要我和一只熊去争洞穴，我会出洋相的；我也相信，出洋相的并非我一人。

然而人类之间的竞争，人与人，团体与团体，依然在进行着，而且和以前一样激烈。

众所周知，凡是白人侵入原始文化的地方，破坏作用最大的不是杀人的武器，而是思想。

当你生活在一个社会当中的时候，社会的风俗习惯会严格地制约你，使你很难有破坏性的想法。

向现代世界灌输一种思想以便摧毁我们人类是可能的事情，对此我并不怀疑。

我们不能脱离我们大脑所限定的模式去思考问题，我们只能稍微离开一点，就这也需要我们有独创的思想。

你一定熟读的

情景模拟对话一

A: Is there a lot of crime in your city?

B: There's some, but I don't think it's a big problem. A lot of it is petty crime, burglary and car theft. There's very little major crime.

A: It's the same in my city. We also have a lot of drug addicts. A lot of the crime is committed by drug addicts who need money for drugs.

B: That happens in many places. In my city, there is a very good drug rehabilitation program. The police and courts are also tough on people who commit crimes, but I don't know if that's the reason for our relatively low crime rate.

A: Some people believe that a tough approach is better. Others prefer a more lenient approach.

B: I think that the best way to reduce crime is to spread wealth more evenly. If most people have similar amounts of money, they will not think of stealing from others.

A: That's possible, but I'm not sure it would really happen like that.

A: 在你的城市，有很多犯罪案吗？

B: 有一些，但是我觉得不是很大的。大部分都是小的罪行，像盗窃和偷车，没有什么大的罪行。

A: 我们这也是一样。我们这儿还有大批的吸毒者。很多犯罪案都是，吸毒成瘾的人都是需要钱来买毒品。

B: 在很多地方都是那样。在我们那里，有一个很好的戒毒计划，警察和法院对犯罪的人同样严厉。但是我不知道这个是不是我们这犯罪率相对较低的原因。

A: 有些人认为，一个强硬的方法是更好的。另一些人喜欢更宽松的方法。

B: 我认为最好减少犯罪的方法是使财富更加平衡。如果大多数人都有差不多的钱，他们就不会想着偷别人的了。

A: 可能吧，但我不确定是否真能发生那样的情况。

情景模拟对话二

A: Which social problem do you think the government needs to concentrate on most?

B: I think housing is a big problem. There are thousands of homeless people on the streets.

A: How would you solve the problem?

B: I have a good idea to solve it. The government could provide some money for homeless people to build their own homes.

A: It would probably be very expensive.

B: I think the government can afford it. Besides, there are many advantages. Homeless people would find it easier to get jobs if they had an address. They would learn some useful skill for finding jobs in the construction industry or home improvement.

A: It's not a bad idea. I think education is the biggest problem at the moment. Schools don't seem to have enough money to educate kids properly.

B: If we are to invest more money to education, we will need to raise taxes. That wouldn't be popular with voters.

A: Most voters want the government to pay for lots of things, but without increasing taxes.

B: The government should show that it is using money efficiently. Sometimes you hear about how the government has wasted money on a project.

A: Yes. The government has limited funds and must show that it is using the money responsibly.

A: 你认为哪个是政府需要更加集中关注的社会问题？

B: 我认为住房是一个大问题。大街上有成千上万的无家可归的人。

A: 你如何解决这个问题呢？

B: 我有一个好想法来解决它。政府可以提供些钱给无家可归的人建立自己的家园。

A: 这可能是非常昂贵的。

B: 我认为政府能负担得起。除此之外，还有许多优势。如果无家可归的人有一个地方的话，他们会发现更容易找到工作。他们可以为找到关于建筑业或家具装饰上的工作学到一些有用的技巧。

A: 这是个不错的主意。我认为教育是最大的问题。学校似乎没有足够的钱来教育孩子。

B: 如果我们要投入更多的资金来教育，我们将需要增加税收。那就不会受选民欢迎。

A: 大多数选民希望政府能付很多东西，但不增加税收。

B: 政府应该表现出它有效地使用金钱。有时，你听到关于政府如何在一个项目上浪费金钱。

A: 是的。政府已经资金有限，必须表现出用这笔钱是负责任的。

你最好掌握的

1 petty /ˈpeti/ a. 琐碎的，小规模的，小气的
2 burglary /ˈbəːɡləri/ n. 盗窃行为
3 addict /əˈdikt/ v. 使……沉溺，使……上瘾 n. 沉溺者，上瘾者
4 commit /kəˈmit/ v. 委托（托付），犯罪，作……事，承诺
5 rehabilitation /ˈriː(h)əbiliˈteiʃən/ n. 复原；修复
6 tough /tʌf/ a. 强硬的，艰苦的，棘手的，严厉的
7 relatively /ˈrelətivli/ ad. 比较地，相对地
8 lenient /ˈliːnjənt/ a. 宽大的，仁慈的
9 evenly /ˈiːvənli/ ad. 平衡地，平坦地，平等地
10 amount /əˈmaunt/ n. 数量，总额 v. 总计，等于，合计

180

11 improvement /im'pru:vmənt/ *n*. 改良，改进，改善；增进；提高；增值

12 properly /'prɔpəli/ *ad*. 适当地，相当地，当然地

13 limited /'limitid/ *a*. 有限的

Lesson

46

Hobbies

 你必须背诵的

业余爱好

烦恼是感情的发作，此时脑子纠缠住了某种东西又不肯松手。

对一个从事社会活动的人来说，培养一种业余爱好和各种新的兴趣是头等重要的做法。

要想在需要的时候可随手摘取充满生机的果实，那就必须从精选良种做起。

一个人要真想感到幸福和平安，至少应该有两三种爱好，而且都比较实际。

他们到处狂奔乱跑，企图以闲聊和乱窜来摆脱无聊对他们的报复，但这是徒劳的。

说实在的，把工作当作享受的那些人可能最需要每隔一段时间把工作从头脑中撇开。

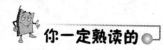你一定熟读的

情景模拟对话一

A: What do you do in your free time, Ping?

B: Well, I like shopping and I play badminton at the weekends.

A: Badminton?

B: Yes, I like badminton a lot. What about you? What do you like doing in your free time?

A: Me? Well, I like going to the cinema and the theatre. And I like reading books and I play the guitar in a band.

B: Wow! You have a lot of hobbies.

A: Well, I like to enjoy my free time.

A: 平，你业余时间做什么？

B: 周末，我喜欢购物还有打羽毛球。

A: 羽毛球？

B: 是啊，我特喜欢羽毛球。你呢？你的业余爱好又是什么呢？

A: 我吗，我喜欢看电影和戏剧，我也喜欢读书，另外，我还在乐队里弹吉他。

B: 真的！你有这么多的业余爱好啊。

A: 是，我喜欢享受自己的业余时间。

情景模拟对话二

A: Do you have any hobbies? What is it or what are they?

B: I am interested in watching TV or other relaxing games.

A: How do you spend your spare time?

B: I usually read or do some sports.

A: What kind of books are you interested in?

B: My favorite books are those about detectives.

A: Well, those books are really good. I like them too. Do you think you are introverted or extroverted?

B: In fact, I wouldn't call myself extroverted. Sometime I enjoy being by myself very much. But other times, I like sharing activities with others too, especially during these last few years.

A: What kind of sports do you like?

B: I like almost all sports, and I enjoy both playing and watching. I especially like tennis and mountain climbing.

A: What kind of personality do you think you have?

B: Well, I approach things very enthusiastically, I think, and I don't like to leave anything half-done. It makes me nervous, I can't concentrate on anything else until the first thing is finished.

A: 你有什么爱好吗? 他们是什么?

B: 我对看电视挺感兴趣, 还有就是一些放松的游戏。

A: 你的业余生活是什么?

B: 通常看书或者做运动。

A: 你对什么类型的书感兴趣?

B: 是关于侦探类的书。

A: 嗯, 这样的书是不错, 我也喜欢, 你觉得你是个外向还是内向的人?

B: 事实上, 我不能说自己外向, 因为有时我很享受自己独处的时间。但有时我也喜欢和别人参加一些活动特别是过去的几年。

A: 你喜欢什么样的运动?

B: 我什么运动都喜欢, 我既喜欢去玩也喜欢观看。我特别喜欢网球和爬山。

A: 你觉得你是什么性格的人?

B: 嗯, 我对事情都很有激情, 我想, 我不喜欢半途而废。这样我会很焦虑。如果第一件事情没做完, 我会没办法集中注意力去做其他事情。

你最好掌握的

1 badminton /ˈbædmintən/ *n*. 羽毛球

2 spare /speə/ *a*. 多余的，备用的，薄弱的 *v*. 节省，节约；抽出，分给；省去，免除；饶恕 *n*. 备用零件

3 introverted /ˈintrəvɜːtid/ *a*. (性格) 内向的

4 extroverted /ˈekstrəvɜːtid/ *a*. 性格外向的

5 approach /əˈprəutʃ/ *v*. 靠近，接近，动手处理 *n*. 途径，方法

6 enthusiastically /inˌθjuːziˈæstikəli/ *ad*. 热情地

7 concentrate /ˈkɔnsentreit/ *v*. 集中，专心，注意，浓缩

8 nervous /ˈnɜːvəs/ *a*. 紧张的，神经失常的，害怕的

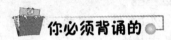

大 逃 亡

图省钱是露营的一个主要动机，因为除了开始时购置或者租借一套露营装备外，总费用算起来要比住旅馆开支少得多。

现代露营装备一年比一年讲究，这对那些愤世嫉俗者来说是一件有趣的自相矛盾的事情。

在露营地里根本不会有管人的"人上人"和酒店里的等级制度来使露营者的假日过得阴郁低沉。

他们争论说，心胸狭窄和自我封闭是并存的。但这种说法在受人欢迎的欧洲露营场是站不住脚的。

假日旅馆有只接待来自一个国家的旅游者的倾向，有时会达到排他的程度。

市政当局当然希望获得露营者的场地费和其他光临的好处，警察则对那些查不出有固定营地或住处的游荡者保持警惕。

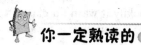
你一定熟读的

情景模拟对话一

A: Just look! It is a lovely day!

B: Yes, it is a good day for a picnic.

A: I was thinking the same thing.

B: Well, how about it then?

A: Okay by me. How soon do you want to leave?

B: Say... in an hour.

A: Make it an hour and a half. We have to take time to get some more food, and besides that I'd like to invite Nancy and Jim.

B: Fine. While you're getting things ready in the house, I'll go to pack them into the car.

A: 看呐! 今天天气多棒啊!

B: 是啊,今天适合去野餐。

A: 我也这么想呢。

B: 好吧,什么时候去呢?

A: 好的,我说,你什么时候能出发?

B: 我想想,一个小时吧。

A: 一个半小时吧. 我们要花点时间去买点东西,然后,我们还要邀请南茜和吉姆一起去。

B: 好. 你在家里准备,我去把东西搬上车子里。

情景模拟对话二

A: That was a great party. Thanks for staying behind to help me clear up.

B: It certainly was a great party. It's a pity that a glass and a plate got broken and someone spilled a drink over there.

A: I expected that something might get broken. That doesn't bother me. That spilled drink won't leave a stain, will it?

B: I doubt it, I'll deal with it right away. Luckily it wasn't a glass of red wine. I'll just get a bowl of water and a cloth.

A: I'm going to put all the rubbish into this big plastic bag.

B: Afterwards, we can do the washing up together. Everything will be finished within an hour. Your friend Keith is really funny. I liked his magic tricks.

A: Yes, he's very good, isn't he? He told some funny stories too.

B: Amanda told some very funny jokes. At the beginning of the party, she was being very serious.

A: I think that she had a little too much of the punch.

B: What did you put in that punch? It tasted great, but was quite strong.

A: That's my little secret. Did you like the snacks and I prepared?

B: Very much. The birthday cake was delicious, wasn't it? Emily told me that she and Karen made it themselves.

A: That cake tasted so good! It disappeared within minutes, so I think everyone liked it a lot. How's that stain?

B: All cleaned up. Are you ready to start on the washing up?

A: 好棒的派对呀，谢谢你留下来帮助我打扫。

B: 这当然是一次精彩的派对，可惜的是打碎了一个杯子和盘子，一些人把酒洒在那边了。

A: 我预料到一些东西会打碎，但是这没有什么。只是那个酒的酒不会留下污点吧？

B: 不敢保证。我会马上处理的。很幸运不是一杯红酒，我这就去拿一碗水还有抹布。

A: 我去把垃圾放进大的塑料袋里。

B: 而后，我们可以一起洗碗。一个小时之内所有事就会完成。你的朋友基斯很有趣，他的魔术我很喜欢。

A: 他是很棒，可是吗？他也讲了一些有意思的故事。

B: 阿曼达告诉我好多有意思的笑话，在派对开始的时候，她还很认真。

A: 我想她有点喝多了。

B: 你往酒里面放了什么? 味道很好, 但是很烈。

A: 这是我的一个小秘密, 你喜欢那些我准备的点心吗?

B: 非常喜欢, 生日蛋糕好吃极了, 不是吗? 艾米莉告诉我是她和凯伦自己做的。

A: 蛋糕的味道好极了, 不过很快就没有了, 我想大家都很喜欢吃吧, 那些污点怎么样了?

B: 所有的都收拾干净了, 你准备洗碗了吗?

 你最好掌握的

1 spill /spil/ v. 溢出, 洒, 使……流出

2 stain /stein/ v. 沾染, 染污, 着色

3 plastic /ˈplæstik, plɑːstik/ a. 塑料的 n. 塑料; 塑料制品

4 expect /iksˈpekt/ v. 预期, 盼望, 期待, 猜想

5 magic trick 魔术

6 punch /pʌntʃ/ n. 酒, 水, 糖等制成的鸡尾酒; 猛击; 冲床 v. 用拳猛击; 打孔

Lesson

48

Planning a share portfolio

 你必须背诵的

规划股份投资

认真的投资者需要一份正规的投资组合表——一种计划很周密的投资选择，结构明确，目标清晰。

没有一种完全"正确"的方法来排列这种投资组合，然而，却毫无疑问地有几种错误的方法。

如果你年纪较大，你从重大投资损失中恢复过来的时间就较少，你就很希望能够提高你的养老金收入。

如果你年轻一些，并且经济状况可靠，你可能会采取一种积极进取的方式——你必须性格开朗，不会因股票价格的浮动而夜不能眠。

一旦你的投资目标确立以后，你就可以决定你的钱投向何处。

 你一定熟读的

情景模拟对话一

A: What's up?

B: I want to invest in stocks to make a quick buck.

A: Really? I'm trading also. So which company are you going to invest in?

B: I think Baidu looks promising, so I'm going to put all my money in it and make a big profit.

A: What? All of your money? Don't put all your eggs in one basket. You need to diversify your portfolio.

B: Really? Thanks for letting me know.

A: 最近忙什么呢?

B: 我想炒股,尽快赚点儿钱花。

A: 是吗? 我也一直炒呢。那你打算买什么股?

B: 我看好百度,打算把钱都放在上面,大赚一笔。

A: 什么? 都投在上面? 千万不要孤注一掷。你应该做多样性的投资组合。

B: 真的? 多谢你告诉我这些。

情景模拟对话二

A: Would you tell me something about stock?

B: Sure, what do you want me to start with?

A: Uhh, you can start with the explanation of some terms like "a bull" and "a bear".

B: OK. A bull is a situation in which share prices are rising.

A: What about a bear, then?

B: A bear is a situation in which share prices keep falling.

A: Oh, I see. But why the prices get rising or falling?

B: If there are more buyers, the price will rise. Otherwise, the price will be lower and lower.

A: How can we make money in the stock market?

B: If you believe the market will go up, you can buy in or hang on. If it turns out to be true, you can make your profit.

A: I heard that some people can earn money out of a bear market. How do they win in such a situation?

B: If you believe the market will fall down, you can sell out your shares and then buy back at a lower price. The price difference is your profit.

A: It sounds easy to make money from stock investment.

B: Not at all. When you really invest in stock market, you'll get involved into the whole world.

A: What do you mean by that?

B: To decide which share you'll buy in is quite hard sometimes. You have to consider the market tendency, the growth of the company and you'd better know something about technical analysis.

A: So boring it is. I'd better invest in some fixed interest fields.

B: Certainly you can. You won't suffer from the risks. But your wallet will suffer.

A: What should I do?

B: If you really want to invest in stock, perhaps you should find a broker.

A: 你能告诉我一些关于股票的事情吗?

B: 当然了,要我从哪儿开始讲呢?

A: 嗯,你可以从"牛市"和"熊市"的解释开始吧。

B: 牛市就是指股价上涨。

A: 那熊市呢?

B: 熊市就是股价下跌了。

A: 喔,我知道了,那为什么要上涨和下跌呢?

B: 如果买的人多了,那么价格就会上升,否则,就会越来越低。

A: 那么我们怎么在股市挣钱呢?

B: 如果你相信股价会上涨,你可以买进或者持股不动,如果股价真的上涨了,这时候再把手里的股票卖掉,就可以赚钱了。

A: 还听说有些人在熊市也能获利,他们是怎么做的呢?

B: 如果你相信市场会跌,你可以卖掉所有的股份然后以低价再买回来。而差价就是你的收益。

A: 听起来在股票投资上很容易赚钱。

B: 绝没有听起来那么容易。因为如果你在股市投了资,你也就